The jet roared
Scarlett breathe
as it lifted up into the sky.

"I have two children—" she began.

Aristide frowned, released his belt and plunged upright, wearing an expression of shock at her announcement that she was a mother. She had become a parent with Walker? She had had a child with *him*? That cut something deep in him that he didn't understand, and it hurt like the devil. He couldn't interpret that distorted feeling of loss and betrayal and he took refuge in outrage at the news. *"Two?"* he questioned as that latter fact sank in. "You were barely married a year before his accident! How on earth could you have had two children in that space of time?"

"They're twins," Scarlett almost whispered, knowing that he had once had a twin brother, who had passed away, but knowing little more detail beyond that. "They're eighteen months old, a little boy and a little girl. They're *yours*."

Lynne Graham was born in Northern Ireland and has been a keen romance reader since her teens. She is very happily married to an understanding husband who has learned to cook since she started to write! Her five children keep her on her toes. She has a very large dog who knocks everything over, a very small terrier who barks a lot and two cats. When time allows, Lynne is a keen gardener.

Books by Lynne Graham

Harlequin Presents

The Italian's Bride Worth Billions
The Baby the Desert King Must Claim

Cinderella Sisters for Billionaires

The Maid Married to the Billionaire
The Maid's Pregnancy Bombshell

The Stefanos Legacy

Promoted to the Greek's Wife
The Heirs His Housekeeper Carried
The King's Christmas Heir

Visit the Author Profile page
at Harlequin.com for more titles.

Two Secrets to Shock the Italian

LYNNE GRAHAM

HARLEQUIN®
PRESENTS™

Recycling programs
for this product may
not exist in your area.

ISBN-13: 978-1-335-59342-9

Two Secrets to Shock the Italian

Copyright © 2024 by Lynne Graham

Harlequin Enterprises ULC
22 Adelaide St. West, 41st Floor
Toronto, Ontario M5H 4E3, Canada
www.Harlequin.com

Printed in Lithuania

MIX
Paper | Supporting
responsible forestry
FSC® C021394

Two Secrets to Shock the Italian

CHAPTER ONE

ARISTIDE ANGELICO, BILLIONAIRE FOUNDER of Angelico Technologies and a once legendary playboy, rested back in his limousine as he was ferried to Luke Walker's memorial service. Six feet four inches, he was built like an athlete, lean and muscular in every long line with unruly black curls, bright green eyes and a startlingly handsome face.

He questioned what he was doing.

'Why are you going to this?' his PA had asked him casually that morning. 'You hardly knew the man.'

The answer?

Aristide was attending out of pure, unvarnished curiosity. The death of an innocent cyclist in busy traffic on his very first day of permanent work had ironically made the news. Aristide had been stunned when he recognised the photo.

He had not, however, been keen to see his ex, weeping over the coffin of her late husband. It would all have been a fake show, a demonstration of the reality that she had about as much emotional depth as a puddle. So, he had ducked the funeral, choosing to attend the memorial service instead.

Aristide had Scarlett Pearson, the dewy-eyed primary schoolteacher, in his bed for almost a year and he had believed he knew her inside out. But, surprise, surprise, he reflected cynically, he had proved to be just as foolishly trusting as many men when it came to a tiny, beautiful redhead. Certainly, Aristide had been stunned when, within weeks of becoming inexplicably unavailable, Scarlett had announced—by cowardly text—that she was getting married to Luke Walker. Luke, her *best* friend from childhood, and a relationship that she had repeatedly assured Aristide was pure and platonic.

More fool him for trusting her! In spite of all the precautions Aristide had taken to keep himself invulnerable, he had ended up almost being a fool for a woman, just as his grandfather and father had been, just as his late twin brother, Daniele, had been. The Angelico men had a poor track record with the opposite sex. As a teenager, Aristide had sworn to remain a playboy and for years that resolve had held fast. The golden years of youth, ignorance and irresponsibility, he labelled that period now. He was only twenty-nine, but he had been a stud at eighteen, determined never to tie his future to either a cold-hearted shrew like his mother or to a cheating gold-digger as his unfortunate younger brother had.

And now the world was threatening to turn full circle, he acknowledged grimly. His mother was putting pressure on him to marry years before he was ready to embrace the institution. Why was he even listening to her? Unfortunately, Daniele's last heartbreaking request of his brother had been that Aristide strive to be kinder and more understanding of their mother's unpleasant nature. It was a tall order, but Aristide was still attempting to be tolerant out of respect for his late twin's memory and to make allowances for his mother's tragic past.

'For the sake of the family,' Daniele had urged, because family had meant everything to his twin... sadly, a great deal less to Aristide.

Suitable marital prospects were served up to Aristide at every family event he attended, and it had become seriously annoying. After all, his plan had always been to stay single until he was middle-aged. Only then would he marry to provide the next generation. He had no perfect candidate in mind, but then he didn't believe a perfect woman existed. He had, however, already considered the desirable attributes his wife should possess. She would have to be beautiful, wealthy in her own right and of a maternal nature. That last trait was non-negotiable. Nobody knew better than Aristide what it had been like to grow up with a cold, cruel mother.

'You're exhausted,' Edith, Scarlett's mother-in-law, sighed in a sympathetic undertone in the church foyer, scanning the younger woman's shadowed eyes.

'You are as well,' Scarlett pointed out ruefully as

she acknowledged that the sudden unexpected death of her husband a year earlier had ripped the heart out of the whole family circle.

Luke had essentially died in a cycling accident on the way to work, only the shell of him had lingered in a hospital bed for two long months afterwards. There had, however, been no real hope that he would emerge from his coma during those dreadful weeks and eventually she and her in-laws had agreed for the machines keeping him alive to be switched off. He had been twenty-four years old, newly qualified as an accountant and a much-loved only child with everything to live for still ahead of him. And in the blink of an eye he was now gone and nothing could change that reality.

Scarlett dragged in a ragged breath.

She was empty of tears now. The weeks during which Luke had lain unresponsive in his hospital bed had drained her of the first sobbing desperation of grief. In addition, she was no stranger to family loss. Her adoptive parents had died soon after her marriage, one from a long-standing illness, the other from a massive stroke, brought on, she suspected, by the shock of bereavement. Becoming an adult orphan had made Scarlett even more grateful to have Luke and his parents in her corner. He had helped her build their family with *two* parents. Now, without Luke around to steady her, she felt as though the foundation of her world had collapsed and she knew that she had to get over feeling that way because she still had two young children to raise.

Just about the very last thing Scarlett was prepared to handle was the shocking vision of her ex, Aristide, striding up the path to the church door where she and Luke's parents were greeting their friends. Impossibly elegant in a dark suit, so beautifully tailored it could only have hailed from an Italian designer, Aristide Angelico looked utterly untouched by the passage of time. Not that that surprised her, because she had learned the hard way that nothing much touched Aristide deep and it *had* only been two years since she had last seen him. That two years for her, however, had been packed tight with her pregnancy, her marriage, the birth of her twins and a new life darkened by the loss of Luke, but an utterly different life from what she had once had while she was with Aristide.

Gleaming black curls that caught the sunlight and were a little too long for tidiness tumbled above a lean, stunningly handsome face. Aristide was a male whom few women failed to notice. Scarlett could feel her knees weakening as though some insidious spell had entered her bloodstream the instant she saw him. It brought back bad memories of how lost she had once got in Aristide, of how vulnerable she had become in the grip of her fear of losing him. And that disturbing surge of recollection hit her at the exact right moment and put her back in control as he grasped Edith's hand, bowed his gorgeous dark head in polite acknowledgment of the sad occasion and murmured conventional words of regret. And then it was Scarlett's turn…

She collided reluctantly with glittering emerald-green eyes as cutting as diamond blades and she didn't hear what he said, didn't even register his hand gripping hers briefly because she *felt* the burning animosity and scorn powering his gaze down into her very bones. Her pale heart-shaped face flamed as though a blowtorch had been turned on her. Involuntarily, she took a tiny step back from him as he turned to address Luke's father, Tom.

Still in shock at being exposed to the passionate aura of charisma that Aristide emanated like a force-field, Scarlett had to be prompted by Edith's hand on her arm to swivel back and greet the next person approaching. Her brain, her very consciousness and control, still, however, seemed lost to her.

She was remembering what she didn't want to remember: Aristide, smiling, concerned and effortlessly captivating the very first time she had met him when she had turned an ankle out jogging. She had not believed that love at first sight existed until that day. The attraction had been *that* instant and overpowering. By the time she truly understood *who* he was, *what* that wealth and status meant in the world and *how* it would colour his every expectation of *her*, she had already been in too deep to pull back. Loving Aristide had made her too forgiving in that she had kept on making excuses for him when he'd disappointed her. No, *no*, she told herself angrily, not going there now, not today, which was her best friend Luke's day…

Aristide sank fluidly down in a pew, his attention locked on the grieving widow's profile. That porcelain-clear skin of hers showed everything. Even though months had passed since her husband's death, she still looked pale, dark shadows bruising her remarkably blue eyes, her skin wildly outclassed in brilliance by the dark auburn fall of hair like molten copper, which she had restrained in an ugly bun. Surprisingly, he wasn't as pleased to see Scarlett still looking wretched as he had assumed he would be. Did that mean that he was a kinder person than he had ever believed he was? He didn't think so.

Once again, he thought how fortunate it was that he had made himself let Scarlett go in every way. He hadn't spied on her from a distance, keeping tabs on her life. Oh, yes, he had been tempted, because curiosity could be a killer, but he had known that ultimately it was better for him simply to turn his back and move on without wondering how her new life with another man might be developing.

Even so, questions were still bubbling up like burning lava in the back of his mind, the sort of questions he had suppressed two years earlier, questions that he considered *beneath* him. Had she always loved Luke Walker? Had she set up Aristide as a rival to inspire jealousy and finally win her best friend's sexual interest? Or had she been cheating on Aristide all along? In one of those twisted can't-commit-can't-let-you-go relationships?

But she *had* been a virgin, not that Aristide had ever chosen to openly acknowledge that fact lest he encourage his lover to have expectations. And he never ever made that mistake with women. He was always very clear about what he was and what he *wasn't* offering. She had accepted the status quo just as all the women he had ever met did. Even so, Scarlett had continually strained against the boundaries of that acceptance. She had refused expensive gifts and holidays, refused to acknowledge that his needs as the CEO of an international business empire should naturally take precedence over her own humbler calling. Indeed, Scarlett had sometimes been so blasted difficult that he had wondered why he was still with her.

Even so, Aristide was no fool. Scarlett Pearson/ Walker still intrigued him because she had ditched *him* and she was the only female who had *ever* walked away from him. Of course, that fact still rankled with a guy whom Scarlett had once accused of having an ego as big as the planet. It was natural for him to wonder why she had picked another man, nothing more complex than that.

He attended the community-hall sandwiches-and-tea gathering that followed the memorial service. He had rarely felt so out of his depth anywhere, listening to impromptu speeches being made about Luke

Walker, who had apparently been a noted youth and outreach volunteer in the local church and various organisations. A Mr Perfect, Aristide decided, wondering what murky secrets Scarlett's husband had been hiding below that squeaky-clean surface because Aristide was that much of an innate cynic.

He couldn't imagine Scarlett with a man like that, but he could imagine her *admiring* a man like that, which set his teeth on edge. When he had first met her, Scarlett's every free hour had seemed to be devoted to similar philanthropic interests, he recalled belatedly, only she had slowly fallen away from all that do-gooding once he pointed out that she was never available when he wanted to see her. Without warning though, Aristide was inexplicably feeling as though he had never really known Scarlett at all and it annoyed him that in many ways he had refused to acknowledge the kind of world she had grown up in. A settled, conventional and conservative realm, which he could barely comprehend because it was the very opposite of the hyper-sophistication, the cold silences and the bitter secrets and dramas that had soiled his own far more dysfunctional background.

Aristide didn't know what family warmth and support was. From what he had witnessed over the years, his parents had *always* detested each other. His father, who had proved to be a most reluctant father and husband in reality, was indifferent to him. His mother, however, idolised him, her sole surviving child, while

Aristide quietly despised and avoided her. Regardless of those unpleasant facts, maintaining the Angelico family line entailed presenting an appearance of unity, dignity and doing one's duty. Aristide, however, had only ever truly cared about one other person and that person had been his beloved twin, who had taken his own life six years earlier. A world shorn of Daniele's bright optimistic spirit still seemed like a very bleak place, but it had somehow felt a little less bleak while Scarlett was by his side.

As Aristide approached her through the gathered cliques of guests, Scarlett froze because, prior to that moment, seated with Luke's parents, she had been covertly watching Aristide's every move. In a crowd he was easily spotted by his sheer height and he was even more strikingly noticeable in his immaculate business attire with an expensive gold watch and cuff-links on display.

Everyone around him was ordinary and Aristide Angelico had never been ordinary even at birth, born as he had been into a fabulously wealthy Italian business dynasty. A monogram AA would be stamped on all his handmade apparel like the shirt she still had somewhere in her belongings. And he was gorgeous, unbelievably, impossibly gorgeous. That was a stray thought she suppressed as soon as it came into her mind as she concentrated on wondering instead why he had attended the service when he hadn't, as far as she knew, attended the funeral.

After all, Aristide must've met Luke in passing a dozen times without ever showing the smallest real interest in her best friend. No doubt he would have exerted himself to be a little more charming had her best friend been a woman. Although he had never voiced a word of criticism or sought to interfere, she had eventually worked out that Aristide didn't like her having a close friend the same sex as himself. By then, she had become adept at recognising what annoyed Aristide, bringing a cool light to his shrewd gaze or a faint curl to his lip or even a very subtle edged intonation. In fact, so good had she become at reading Aristide, she could have written a book about him long before she broke up with him.

'May I have a brief word?' Aristide enquired, smooth as glass.

Scarlett rose from her seat, her legs slightly wobbly. 'Of course.' Stepping away from her in-laws, she murmured tightly, 'Why are you here?'

'I was curious.'

Aristide gazed down at her, scanning the slice of porcelain skin exposed only at the throat by the plain dress, wanting to see more, suddenly exasperated that there was no prospect of such a development. Black lashes pitched low over his spectacular eyes, he studied the ripe curve of her soft lips while involuntarily remembering the taste of her.

For a split second he was knocked sideways by the raw arousal shooting a lightning pulse into his groin. It was inappropriate, wrong, tasteless, everything he was *not* and it outraged his powerful pride. He didn't *still* want her, of course he didn't! It was some crazy throwback to the past combined with unwelcome memories, he reasoned fiercely. But possibly a shot of unvarnished lust was painfully overdue, he conceded, considering that he had not been with a woman in a very long time.

'Why would you be curious?' Scarlett asked in seemingly genuine surprise. 'What would you be curious about?'

A current of pure rage rippled through Aristide, who prided himself on never ever losing his temper. She was playing games with him, of course she was, but what other option did he have other than to play?

'Why you walked away,' he pronounced with gritty reluctance.

Scarlett stared back at him in apparent wonderment, sapphire-blue eyes widening. 'Surely that was obvious?' she responded flatly, turning away as someone else addressed her.

Obvious? Not to Aristide. He wanted an explanation, closure, that was *all*, he assured himself. Clearly, he should have moved on by now, leaving the detritus of that period behind him, but Scarlett had stayed with him like a thorn in tender flesh, nagging at the back of his mind, regardless of how often he threw thoughts of her back out again. He shouldn't have attended the service, he conceded grimly. It was the wrong place, the wrong time.

Feeling drained and yet strung out with nerves, Scarlett finally reclaimed her seat. Edith leant closer and rested a reassuring hand on Scarlett's trembling knees. 'Is that *him*?' she asked very softly. 'He's the living image of our grandkids.'

Scarlett lost colour at that instant recognition while also conceding how very wise and far-seeing Luke had been when he had insisted that there should be no secrets kept from his parents. At the same time, he had admitted that he was gay. 'Yes,' she confirmed flatly because, with their olive skin, black curls and bright green eyes, Rome and Alice were like miniature doppelgängers of their father.

'I'll bring the kids back in an hour,' Edith told Scarlett on the phone. 'They're having fun on the slide. I'll give them lunch and then they can come home and go for a nap, which will give you a break.'

'I don't need another break,' Scarlett pointed out gently. 'I'm not working today.'

'I'm sure you've got stuff round the house to catch up on.'

Indeed, she had, Scarlett conceded as she unloaded

the washing machine and carted the washing out to hang it on the line in the back garden. She was tired but then she had been consistently tired since Luke's passing and she reckoned that that weight of exhaustion could well be part of the grieving process. Her life was harder and lonelier without Luke, but she was very lucky to have a pair of adoring grandparents living in the apartment above theirs.

For the past few weeks, she had been back at work at the primary school where she had been employed since graduation. At present though, she was still only working part-time and once she had got through the summer she would have a better idea as to whether or not she wished to return to full-time hours. Luckily for her, Luke had been well insured when he died and she could have afforded to stay home with the children for a while anyway. At present, however, Scarlett knew she needed the stimulation of work and mixing with other adults to stay on a more even keel.

The Walkers had remodelled their spacious detached home into two apartments and had invited their son and his wife to move into the ground-floor one, believing that the children needed outdoor space more than they did. In reality the two couples and the twins had intermingled to such an extent that the garden was freely shared between them and Edith's husband, Tom, was still tending the garden, finding it a relaxing pastime when he wasn't at his accountancy office.

When the doorbell shrilled, Scarlett frowned because she wasn't expecting anyone and her closest friend, Brie, was at work. Leaving the kitchen, she walked through the narrow hall and pulled open the front door with a smile, assuming that it was a delivery.

Her smile fell away and she froze and took a harried step backwards when she saw who stood on her doorstep. It was Aristide, his green eyes veiled and shrewd as he absorbed her dismay at his sudden appearance. 'I would've phoned to warn you that I was planning a visit but I don't have your current number.'

'Aristide…' she breathed hoarsely, dry-mouthed, throat closing over when she needed to breathe in deep and long to inflate her struggling lungs because the sight of Aristide Angelico at her front door filled her with nothing short of panic.

Her first thought was to thank heaven that the children were out with her mother-in-law and her second was to wonder if she had cleared away the toys in the living room. Of course, there were photos of the children in there as well. Much better to keep him outside, she decided, rigid with discomfiture as she moved out into the fresh air to join him. 'What are you doing here?' she asked stiffly, unable to think of a single reason why he would visit her.

'I'm not prepared to discuss that with you standing out in the garden,' Aristide assured her drily.

Coins of pink sprang up over her cheekbones. With

very poor grace she backed into the apartment again and opened the living-room door, inwardly praying that she had tidied up, stuffing the innumerable clutter that went with raising young children into the plastic toy boxes hidden behind the sofa. To her relief, a clear wooden floor greeted her anxious gaze and she glanced up at Aristide.

He was so much taller than she was that he towered over her. She was four feet eleven inches in her bare feet and she *was* in her bare feet, got up in worn jeans and a T-shirt. She had no make-up on, so her face was bare, and her hair had last been brushed at dawn. Every morning, Rome climbed out of his cot and nagged her out of bed but not before he gave her a big cuddle. He was extremely cuddly for a little boy sired by a non-cuddling father.

'I asked you a question when we last met. It wasn't the right place or time, for which I apologise, but I would still like to hear an answer,' Aristide outlined.

Scarlett could hardly believe her ears. 'It's been two years, Aristide. Why would you come and ask me now?'

'Is there harm to you in me asking that question?' An ebony brow lifted.

'You've got to admit that it's more than a little strange when you didn't care enough at the time to seek me out,' Scarlett countered tightly, fingers snapping into fists by her side. 'But it's no big secret. It was Cosetta Ricci and that big formal ball you took her to in London. You didn't mention it to me, you didn't explain it. She was the last straw. I could hardly compete with a model and an heiress, and I wasn't prepared to *try* and compete either.'

'I never said that we were exclusive—'

'And the minute I realised that we definitely *weren't* exclusive, I wanted out,' Scarlett completed without embarrassment.

'You didn't want out. You wanted to marry your best friend,' Aristide quipped without expression, emerald-green eyes lethal as knives hitting a target.

'I've given you the explanation that you said that you wanted,' Scarlett retorted flatly. 'Now you can leave—'

'Cosetta Ricci,' Aristide repeated in disbelief. 'She meant nothing to me—'

'Neither did I,' Scarlett slotted in before she could think better of making that point. Goodness knew, she had not had a problem working out that hard fact when she'd never heard from him again after that text. He hadn't fought for her, hadn't confronted her, hadn't argued with her, he had simply let her go.

'She was a friend, nothing more. It was a fundraiser sponsored by the Angelico charitable trust and my mother invited Cosetta to attend as my partner—'

A fine brow elevated in unforgiving doubt. 'Like you couldn't have said no! Please leave now,' Scarlett urged thinly, walking back out to the hall to yank the front door open in invitation.

Aristide took the hint but came to a sudden halt on the doorstep to proclaim in seething disbelief, 'You're seriously trying to tell me that Cinderella didn't get asked to the ball and that that's why you walked away and married another man?'

Her face hot as fire, Scarlett slammed the door in his face and stalked back to the kitchen to pace in angry circles of frustration. There was so much she could have said to him, so many good reasons that she had made the choices she had, that he would still have been standing there at midnight had she actually started to talk. But she didn't owe Aristide any humiliating truths or insights into her behaviour, she didn't owe him anything!

In fact, she had done him a *huge* favour. She hadn't saddled him with children he didn't want and a society scandal when word of their out-of-wedlock birth inevitably escaped. The Angelico family and Aristide, in particular, were never out of the newspapers in Europe and their every move attracted publicity.

Scarlett, however, had never been good enough for Aristide or his posh family. He had kept her well away from them until his mother had sought her out at a party and had cruelly mocked her for her working-class background and supposedly unknown parentage as an adopted child. Elisabetta Angelico had made it painfully clear that Scarlett was the lowest of the low in her eyes and no more than a passing fling in her son's life.

In actuality, Scarlett had long known who her birth parents were. Schoolkids, they had moved on with their lives quite happily after surrendering her at birth. Her birth mother, whom she had met at eighteen, enjoyed a high-powered career in fashion and had had little interest in pursuing an ongoing relationship with the daughter she had given up. Her birth father had died in a motorbike crash in his twenties. Her exploration of her true beginnings had been a dead end when it came to establishing the new family connection she had secretly craved. And that had been the direct result of the fact that she had had nothing whatsoever in common with the adoptive parents whom she had, nevertheless, deeply loved.

The following week, Aristide returned to Scarlett's home a second time. He was annoyed that he had not been able to resist the temptation to see her again, impatient to satisfy the curiosity she inspired but equally keen to walk away again, miraculously cured of what was beginning to feel like an obsession. He hit the doorknocker and heard footsteps approaching. The door opened on Scarlett's slender blonde mother-in-law. Unexpectedly, the older woman smiled in welcome. 'Mr Angelico. I'm afraid Scarlett's at work but she finishes for the day in fifteen minutes.'

A very young child lurched up and hugged her leg and then another one appeared to hug her other leg, two upturned little faces staring up at Aristide with huge curious eyes. There was something about the duo, something about their faces, that was weirdly familiar.

Frowning, Aristide asked where Scarlett worked and if he could have her phone number to warn her that he was coming to pick her up. Both his queries were answered pleasantly. There appeared to be no awareness that he had ever been anything other than a casual friend of Scarlett's and for some reason that annoyed him. But then, for several months, Aristide had recognised that he was out of sorts, awash with impulsive responses that were as much out of character as the restlessness afflicting him. For a disciplined, unemotional male, that lack of control was maddening.

He wondered vaguely who the children belonged to as he swung back into the limo and directed his driver to the school. He texted Scarlett, anticipating her alarm with sudden wicked amusement. He was surprised that she was still working at the same place and equally surprised that she was still apparently living with her in-laws. But then, she had rejected his lifestyle, even his gifts, leaving behind everything he had ever given her when she left him. Clearly, Luke Walker and his family, however, had been exactly what she wanted in her life. As usual, the thought rankled.

He had picked her up at the school before and she had been ridiculously embarrassed because people had stared at the limousine, but when he had turned up in a Ferrari some weeks later, she had been no more pleased. Now he sat watching her stalk down the pavement towards him, a beige raincoat floating back from her narrow shoulders, an even more boring brown skirt and top worn beneath. Her hair was descending in little copper strands from her updo and she was flushed. But dress Scarlett up in designer fashion and, tiny though she was, she was a total showstopper. Involuntarily, he thought what a shame it was that she wouldn't be available to be his partner at his unwelcome thirtieth family birthday party, which he was due to attend in two weeks.

He hadn't asked his parents for the party and he didn't want it. He had considered simply not turning up, a response that would have humiliated his very socially sensitive mother in front of friends and relatives. That no-show option would have been utterly cruel, in his late twin's parlance, and Aristide had gritted his teeth and decided to attend on that basis. On the balance side, however, the sight of Scarlett back in her son's life would wondrously enrage his lady mother and enliven the evening for Aristide, and Scarlett's presence would certainly keep the marriage groupies at bay. And then he thought, well, why shouldn't he ask her? It was not as though he would be asking her to get into a bed with him again.

Scarlett slid into the back of the limo at speed, wanting the opulent car to move off again fast, wanting people to stop staring. She was furious with Aristide, furious that he had contrived to surprise her. It had always been a mistake to second-guess Aristide, to underestimate what he was capable of when he was challenged. But she hadn't challenged him, hadn't done anything to reanimate his interest or his wretched curiosity!

'What on earth are you doing here?' she demanded as she turned to look at him.

And the impact of Aristide that close engulfed her like an avalanche. Bright green eyes clear as water against smooth bronzed skin, cheekbones sharp enough to cut glass, a wide sensual mouth set in a sculpted jawline dark with stubble. Drop-dead gorgeous at any time of day but even more stunning when seen without warning and after the passage of time.

Only two years, she reminded herself afresh, but it seemed more like a lifetime since her fingers had last tingled with an overwhelming desire to touch him. *Touch* the silky black curls that tangled round her fingers, *smooth* away the frown etched between his level dark brows, *trace* the sultry, sexy shape of his lips. Being that near Aristide after so long shook her inside out with guilty longing.

'I have something you left behind—'

'Stick it in the post,' Scarlett urged tightly.

'As it was something precious to you, I didn't like to risk it,' Aristide drawled.

His dark deep voice vibrated down her spine and travelled into more intimate territory. She shivered and froze rigid, Aristide still in her mind's eye even though she was no longer allowing herself to look at him. Aristide in a smooth dove-grey suit, elegantly cut to enhance every line of his lean, powerful body, a white shirt at his bronzed throat, a blue silk tie. He was like catnip and she was the cat, she thought crazily. She couldn't even think about the conversation. Her mind was a blank and her whole body was braced in a defensive position as if she were awaiting an attack.

Aristide studied her, almost wincing as she crossed her slender legs in the pencil skirt and he caught a glimpse of a smooth silken inner thigh. A glimmer of arousal pulsed a warning at his groin and he tensed in immediate denial. He wondered why she was in such a nervous state, why she wouldn't look at him, why she hadn't even asked *what* it was that she had left behind in his apartment. And then he asked himself why he was questioning such random issues and even why he would care what was wrong with her.

The limousine drew up outside his townhouse and the passenger door was opened by his driver. Scarlett's head swivelled. 'Where are we?' she mumbled in confusion.

'At my place. We'll have lunch and talk before I take you home and return to the office,' Aristide murmured in a tone of unnatural calm as if such an idea were perfectly normal.

'We have nothing to talk about!' she gasped.

'You may yet be surprised,' Aristide quipped.

But Scarlett didn't like surprises and her heart sank like a stone because it was entirely possible that Aristide had somehow found out about the children or, at the very least, become suspicious. On wobbly legs, she scrambled out of the limo, her tummy rolling like a ship in high seas, every nerve on overdrive.

CHAPTER TWO

ARISTIDE HAD LIVED in a penthouse apartment when Scarlett had known him. Now she was standing outside a tall Georgian townhouse in one of London's most famous garden squares.

'You've moved?' she breathed, accompanying him up the steps to the front door already standing open on a gracious hallway.

'It was originally my grandfather's property. I inherited it last year after he passed away,' Aristide confided smoothly as an elderly man in the smart dark jacket of a very superior manservant greeted them with great formality at the door.

'James…my guest, Miss Scarlett Pearson—'

'Walker,' Scarlett inserted.

'Mrs Walker,' Aristide conceded very drily. 'I thought you weren't a fan of a woman taking a man's name.'

Scarlett flushed. He was correct. That had been her opinion only until she became pregnant and her adoptive mother had flinched every time she was addressed as 'Miss'. But then that sort of label had been hugely important to her adoptive parents, who would have been heartbroken and mortified had she become pregnant without a respectable husband on the horizon. And Luke, bless him, had stepped up when she needed him to fill that space.

'Why would I have lunch with you?' Scarlett whispered, intimidated by the grandeur of the hall.

Aristide shrugged. 'Why wouldn't you? We didn't part as enemies.'

It was true. There had been no final confrontation, no bitter exchanges. She had expected one, had expected to have to tell lies to support her story. She had dreaded the possibility, imagining Aristide's shrewd and far too clever green eyes digging into her as she voiced those same lies. But Aristide had made no attempt to see her again. He had let her walk away, proving that she meant nothing to him, proving that she had merely been another body in his bed. His indifference had devastated her even while it had best suited her needs at the time.

She was shown into an elegant dining room. Aristide slid her coat off her taut shoulders and passed it to the older man. Drinks were offered. She accepted a moisture-beaded glass of white wine, while striving to recall when she had last enjoyed an alcoholic drink. She watched Aristide like a hawk, trying to work out what he wanted from her. Certainly, he wouldn't be in the market for a list of complaints relating to her departure from his life. He had to have some other motivation to seek her out and she tensed because she had never been able to out-think Aristide.

As she sipped her wine, he dropped a small, worn box down into her lap. She blinked in surprise and then recognition raced through her at speed and she set her drink down hurriedly to open the box. As she had hoped, it was the tiny pearl stud earrings her parents had bought her for her twenty-first birthday.

'*Real* pearls,' her mother had stressed with immense pride.

'I thought I'd lost them!' she exclaimed.

'No, you left them behind. I meant to send them on to you but I forgot about them until I moved in here,' Aristide volunteered, reckoning that she wouldn't thank him for the rest of the stuff she had left behind.

Possibly she didn't want to remember the cobweb-fine lingerie he had bought and she had finally worn for his benefit. She hadn't understood how much he *loved* seeing her in items like that. She had deemed that risqué, like sex in daylight and sex other than in a bed. Once upon a time Scarlett had had a lot of inhibitions and Aristide had had the enjoyable challenge of moulding her into *his* perfect woman. And she had been perfect for months, she had been perfect as long as he sidestepped the awkward questions about where their relationship was heading and any fatal meeting with her parents, which would only have destined her to disappointment. She had wanted more from him, but Aristide had never been with a woman who *didn't* want more from him. It had not occurred to him until it was far too late that Scarlett would leave him sooner than settle for less.

And now she sat there in a little patch of sunlight that suffused her in gold tones. Titian highlights glimmered from her hair, gilding her cheekbones as she smiled at him, delighted to receive her insignificant earrings back. Of course, she had left behind a pair a good deal larger and more valuable, which he had given her. His strong jawline tightened at the memory. No, whatever else he could say about her, Scarlett was not a gold-digger. Not that that had been much of a consolation when she'd suddenly vanished from his life, he conceded grudgingly.

'Thanks,' she said with the first genuine warmth she had shown him as she bent down to tuck that cherished little box into her bag.

'Come and sit down,' he invited, spinning out a chair for her at the table, and he was drowning in memories. Scarlett greeting him with three-course meals when he came home, Scarlett enveloping him in the affection no other woman had ever shown him, Scarlett smiling up at him in bed, so happy, always seemingly so happy that he had been shattered when without warning she told him that she was marrying another man.

Scarlett rose and settled down at the table. 'Was there a reason you wanted to see me?' she dared, stiff as a plank in her seat.

James reappeared and set a tiny ornamental quiche adorned with baby lettuce leaves down in front of her. It was so exquisite a creation that she was almost afraid to touch it. Mouth-watering pastry melted in her mouth and she looked at Aristide enquiringly.

'I have a favour to ask,' Aristide confessed.

Scarlett had braced herself for some reference to her children and her shoulders dropped in relief even as a frown line indented her brow, because Aristide Angelico didn't ask for favours. Other people asked *him* for favours, but Aristide wanted very little and what he did want he *bought*.

'A favour…from me?' she questioned in surprise.

'My parents are holding a thirtieth-birthday bash for me in two weeks and I need a partner. I'd be very grateful if you would agree to accompany me to the party.'

Blue eyes widening, Scarlett gazed back at him, almost stunned into silence. 'Are you serious?'

'Deadly serious.'

'But why me?'

'Because you wouldn't read anything deeper into the invitation,' Aristide returned smoothly. 'It would be strictly platonic. Essentially, you would shield me from all the wannabes my mother will serve up for my appreciation. She's desperate for me to get married… and I'm not in any hurry—'

'At our one meeting it was clear that your mother despised me, so I should be the last person you would ask,' Scarlett pointed out, although she wondered why she was even bothering to make the point since there was no prospect of her accepting his invite.

'No, it makes you the best option,' Aristide countered with a grim smile. 'I don't mind annoying my mother and your reappearance in my life will shock her and persuade her to back off…at least for a while.'

Scarlett shrugged awkwardly and pushed away her empty plate. 'I couldn't do it—'

'The school term is due to finish. You will be on holiday,' Aristide reminded her evenly. 'It will only be for a weekend.'

Scarlett went pink, thinking how very deeply ironic it was that Aristide should finally be inviting her to a family event now that they were no longer in a relationship. Italy was essentially his home, but he had only once taken her to Rome for a weekend. Of course, he would never have asked her to socialise with his parents while they were still together lest she begin dreaming of wedding rings. The sole reason she had met Elisabetta Angelico was that the older woman had sought her out to satisfy *her* curiosity and shoot her down in flames.

'I'm sorry I couldn't do it,' she told Aristide flatly, thinking of Rome and Alice because she was no longer free to come and go as she pleased. In addition, could she spend more time with Aristide without making an accidental slip about the fact that she was now the mother of two toddlers?

'Think it over. Thirty-six hours in the Italian sunshine and naturally I would cover any and all expenses.'

The main course arrived. Scarlett concentrated on her food because she had nothing more to say. She was grateful for the return of her earrings, but she could not see any reason why she would want to spend time with Aristide again. He had hurt her too much. He was a mistake she needed to keep firmly in her past. Although, how could she think of her children as a mistake when they had brought her so much happiness? And without Aristide, she wouldn't even have Rome and Alice, she reminded herself.

Aristide studied her down-bent head while she ate only a single mouthful of the chocolate mousse dessert that was an old favourite of hers. He couldn't even get a conversation out of her and just at that moment he was reluctant to rake up their incendiary past to provide useful fodder. Her quietness called to mind how silent she had become during the last weeks of their affair. Quiet, *secretive*, he had later decided in disgust, although whatever she was hiding from him had not kept her out of his bed or made her any less keen to be with him. No, her unexpected unavailability had only begun during that final month and a flood of lame excuses had come his way: illness, family occasions, work events, relatives and friends visiting.

'I should be going,' Scarlett remarked stiffly. 'I'm

supposed to be going shopping with my mother-in-law this afternoon.'

Aristide gritted his teeth, discovering that her reluctance merely sharpened his desire to spend more time with her. That kneejerk reaction incensed him.

'A break would do you good,' he murmured softly, waving away the coffee tray James held in the doorway.

Unexpected tears stung the backs of Scarlett's eyes because Aristide could sound so considerate, but it was a superficial level of caring. Once he had comforted her when she'd wept over the return of her father's cancer following several operations, but Aristide would neither go to the hospital with her nor visit her parents' home. He had always carefully avoided doing anything that might suggest that their relationship had any real staying power. He had kept her at a distance, shut her out, refusing to even explain why he had little time for his own family.

Determined not to respond, Scarlett rose from her chair and gathered up her bag. 'Don't you need to get back to work?' she muttered in desperation.

'I decide my own schedule.' Aristide vaulted upright, interrupted in the rousing recollection of the hot, tight embrace of her body and thoroughly irritated by his own susceptibility when his quarry wasn't even making a tiny effort to attract him.

'You should go to Italy with him,' Edith Walker recommended, sharply disconcerting Scarlett the evening of the same day. 'Use it as the perfect opportunity to tell him about Rome and Alice.'

Scarlett was stunned by that advice. 'I can't believe you're even suggesting that.'

'Some day you will *have* to tell your children the truth of their parentage and their father has a right to that same information. You can't ignore the facts for ever.' The older woman sighed ruefully. 'Luke's not here to be hurt now and, sadly, Rome and Alice no longer have a father. Even if Mr Angelico was only marginally interested in the twins, he would surely be better than no father at all.'

Scarlett had paled. She was shaken by that frank opinion.

Edith rested a reassuring hand down on hers. 'We wouldn't be having this conversation if my son were still alive. Luke adored being a father. I would have waited a few years before saying these things to you both, but everything has changed and now your ex has brought himself back into the picture, I think it's time for him to be told the truth.'

'Aristide won't *want* to know.'

'If that's true, then your honesty will still have been for the best. You will know where you stand and will be able to advise the children accordingly in the future. If you do this favour for Mr Angelico, he should be better disposed towards you. Try to keep the relationship civil.' Edith sighed. 'But be prepared for him to be very angry that he is only now being told about the twins. A young man as blessed by advantage as he has been in life will be unfamiliar with the sensation of being blindsided.'

Scarlett went to bed that night with a lot on her mind. As the older woman had reminded her, Luke's death had changed everything. For the first time she was being made to recognise that her children had rights too, rights that it would be wrong to ignore. They deserved to know exactly who they were even if it was only out of a desire to receive an accurate medical background.

In the future would Rome and Alice want to know Aristide and his relatives? In staying silent, she reflected, she had overlooked half of their DNA inheritance and the whole family that were part of that. For an instant she felt quite sick at the prospect of confessing what she had concealed from Aristide two years earlier.

But how much would her secret really matter to him? Aristide had never appeared even mildly interested in children and had been reluctant to discuss his opinion of them. At the time she had suspected that he felt that she had no right to ask such personal questions and instead she had read between the lines, as no doubt intended. He had quipped that he didn't want offspring until he was at least fifty and had casually referred to having had to contest two separate paternity claims in the years prior to their meeting, both ultimately proving to be false.

Furthermore, he had never taken the smallest risk with contraception. Even though she had been taking the pill, he had still utilised his own precautions. Aristide gave no woman his full trust. Scarlett still had not the slightest idea how the twins had been conceived. She hadn't missed any pills and hadn't suffered any illness or taken any medication that could have interfered with her birth control. But even so, one morning she had woken up early feeling as sick as a dog and the writing had been on the wall. She had been terrified, not only at the threat of an unplanned pregnancy but also at what such a development would do to her relationship with Aristide.

Wallowing in the past, however, wasn't doing her any favours, she castigated herself, and she sat up in bed to switch on the light and reach for her phone before she could lose her nerve. If she had to tell Aristide that he was a father, it would, she was convinced, be easier to do it when their children were fully out of sight and hearing. She would tell him in Italy. Edith had made it clear that she and Tom would be happy to keep the twins that weekend.

She texted him.

I will go to Italy.

Aristide, working late, reached for his phone and a wide smile lit up his lean dark features. It was two o'clock in the morning and he bet she hadn't noticed the time. Scarlett could be a very anxious little creature. She would've lain awake in bed fretting about his invitation, weighing up pros and cons but, ultimately, choosing the kindest option. Only that once with that unforgettable text had she not been kind or caring with him, he recalled bleakly. He knew her well enough to picture her lying nibbling at her lower lip, brow indented, troubled eyes flickering. She had done a lot of late-night stressing in silence before they parted, he conceded more reflectively. Exactly what had she been worrying about?

You won't regret it.

And she wouldn't, he swore to himself. All of a sudden instead of dwelling on the past and his disillusionment with her, Aristide was recklessly awash with good intentions. He would be a complete gentleman, he decided. Just like one of those stupid, perfect knights in the fairy tales she liked to read to children. Unluckily for him, a steady diet of that kind of conditioning and refinement had not prepared Scarlett for a normal contemporary guy with flaws. Not only would he ensure that he kept his mother well away from her, but if Cosetta Ricci was on the guest list he would keep his distance from her as well rather than offend Scarlett. Energised by such good ideas, Aristide was on a high. He would *protect* Scarlett from any adverse influence. What could possibly go wrong?

* * *

Receiving a text from Aristide early the following morning, Scarlett phoned to ask him, 'What do you mean, there are dresses arriving?'

Aristide groaned, old memories stirring. 'Scarlett, this is an exclusive social event and you won't have anything in your wardrobe that will be suitable. Just imagine being underdressed in my mother's vicinity,' he suggested.

Scarlett shuddered at her end of the phone.

'You're doing this for my benefit, so I will provide the fancy trappings…okay?'

Scarlett heaved a sigh. 'Okay.'

'The seamstress will take your measurements and adjust whatever you choose to a perfect fit and the stylist will provide the clothing.'

'My goodness, you are taking this very seriously.'

'If you feel that you're looking beautiful you will relax and enjoy yourself.'

As she came off the phone, memories wafted Scarlett back in time. Her final year at college she had lived with Brie and two other friends in a smart apartment in Hampstead. The apartment had belonged to Brie's parents, who had been travelling abroad, and Brie had always hated living alone. Scarlett had seen Aristide out jogging several times before she actually met him. She couldn't possibly have kept up the pace he maintained but she had definitely noticed him. Unfortunately, he hadn't seemed like the sort of male who would ever deign to notice her until her foot slid off the kerb one morning and she twisted her ankle and fell. Aristide had come to her rescue. He had picked her up off the pavement…literally picked her up as if she were a doll and carried her into a café to check her ankle.

Someone had arrived with a first-aid kit. She had assumed his security team were his friends. Aristide had even attended to her bleeding knee. He had knelt at her feet and when she'd looked straight into those stunning black-lashed green eyes of his she had been mesmerised, stumbling over her words and giggling when he'd flirted with her. Later she had cringed at that recollection of acting like an airhead. Although she had been sweaty and tousled, it hadn't seemed to matter to him. He had asked her out to dinner that night and just as fast, before she'd even got his name, she had agreed.

'He must live somewhere nearby,' Brie had mused, checking out the name online and then gasping and going into whoops. 'For goodness' sake, Scarlett. If I'd known Aristide Angelico was out there running on the street, I'd have lain in wait for him and tripped him up for myself! Is that him?' she had demanded, angling her phone screen at Scarlett to show Aristide, black curls cropped short, clad in a very sharp suit. 'Honestly? How can you be so lucky?'

And Scarlett had felt like the luckiest girl in the world for those first few dates. Aristide had immense charm and he'd taken her places she could never have afforded to visit alone. She had always been sensible and she had tried to keep her feet on the ground and not allow Aristide's wealth to affect either the way she saw him or the way she behaved with him. She'd also seen his imperfections. He was arrogant and he had the incredibly high expectations of a young man who had never had to settle for less than the best. He was also very reserved and reluctant to talk about his family.

She'd been in the middle of her final exams when he'd asked her to fly out to the Caribbean with him. He had struggled to accept that she had to study and that he had to wait. But in the end, he *had* waited until she was free and she had flown out to Dominica with him for a week and finally shared a bed with him. Secretly she had thought that that intimacy was happening too soon, but she had also known that for the first time ever *she* wanted a man as much as he wanted her and she had gone with her gut instincts and stopped holding back.

'Have a good time with Aristide,' Brie had encouraged. 'But accept up front that it's not going to last. The world's his oyster and he'll move on eventually. Just try not to get hurt.'

With hindsight she wished she had listened more to her friend because Brie had had the experience to recognise that Aristide was not at an age where he wanted to commit to any woman and he ruthlessly guarded his freedom. Scarlett, in contrast, had begun with infatuation and quickly launched into love. Before very long, she had been virtually living in Aristide's apartment when he was in London and she had been moulding her life around him, dropping out of volunteering projects because she'd no longer had the time, telling white lies to her parents to excuse her absences, rather than admit that she was seeing a guy, who winced if she so much as mentioned him meeting her family.

There had been inevitable conflicts between them. Aristide had been continually buying her expensive jewellery and she had given way but only to the extent of wearing the pieces when she was out with him, always knowing that she would leave them behind when they broke up. But when he had asked her to drop everything and fly off somewhere exotic for an occasional week, she had had to say a flat no because she'd valued her job and once the school holidays were over, they were over. Once or twice, he had gone ahead alone, and worrying about what he could be doing without her had killed her pride and much of her resistance.

He'd given her conflicting messages. The night he'd suddenly informed her that they weren't exclusive, she had said, knowing that, if that was true, she had to break up with him, 'So, you're content for me to see other men?'

'No!' he had fired back at her in astonishment, for once losing his cool.

'Well, if it's only you who retains that option then it won't work for me,' she had warned him. 'I'm not the sort of woman who will be content to sleep with you and with other men at the same time. If you want to be with other women, then you don't want to be with *me* and that's fine. The choice is yours.'

And she had returned to Brie's apartment that night in floods of tears knowing that she had had to draw that line in the sand for her own sanity, but heart-broken that he didn't really appreciate what they had together. After all, aside from those occasional fights, Scarlett had been deliriously happy from the moment Aristide had walked into her life and the idea of life without him again had cut her in two.

'You're in too deep with him. Maybe it's better to step away now,' Brie had consoled her.

'If he's already hurting you like this, you're better off without him,' Luke had told her apologetically that same evening.

What had felt like the worst week of Scarlett's life had followed. She had wondered if she had got too caught up in labels and unnerved Aristide. To be fair to him, while she had been with him she had never had the smallest suspicion that there were any other women in his life, but he refused to make an actual promise or a commitment of any kind that might restrict him.

At the end of the week, Aristide had shown up at the door. 'I miss you,' he had admitted stiffly. 'Right now, I don't want anyone else. That is the truth.'

And the silence had hung there while she'd considered that and it had been the uncertain, anxious light in his eyes that had won her over. He hadn't said much, just enough to warm the cold place in her heart. *Right now*, though… Those two words had engulfed her like the crack of doom, reminding her that he didn't see her as figuring in his long-term future. But he had tugged her into his arms and kissed her with a flattering amount of desperation and she had shelved her concerns and insecurities, telling herself that there was always the possibility that she would get bored with him first.

Only in the end it had been the trauma of discovering that she was pregnant that had forced them apart.

CHAPTER THREE

Scarlett certainly wasn't prepared for the arrival of several rails of clothing to be wheeled in for her inspection and the tailor or the bubbly stylist and her assistant who accompanied them. Sadly for her, she was no longer the same size she had been two years earlier, the size Aristide had naively assumed she still was. Pregnancy had changed her shape. She was fuller at breast and hip and no longer rejoiced in quite the same tiny waist.

The tailor, who took her measurements, clicked her teeth in dismay. The twins were mercifully down for a nap and she had Brie with her for a second opinion.

'With your colouring, I would suggest *this* for the big event.' The stylist extended a dream of a dress. The rich emerald shade reminded her of Aristide's eyes. It swept to the floor in beaded, shimmering luxury.

Scarlett swallowed hard and took it across the hall to try it on in privacy. It was rather too tight and she returned to the now cluttered lounge feeling pretty self-conscious.

'That's gorgeous…if you have it in a larger size,' Brie commented.

'It will be specially made to Mrs Walker's exact measurements to ensure a perfect fit,' the tailor assured her.

Accessories were produced and then the shopping experience took on another dimension when outfits were produced for Scarlett to travel in. Thinking that that was excessive, Scarlett excused herself to phone Aristide from the hall.

'How many outfits are you planning to buy me? *Travelling* clothes?' she complained critically.

'The paps are everywhere. I want you to look the part the entire time you're with me. It's no big deal, *bella mia*. It's like a stage role. The clothes are only props.'

Silenced, Scarlett came off the phone again, recalling Edith's advice, which had virtually been to keep Aristide sweet in advance of the shocking news she had to share with him while she was away. Arguing with him would only annoy him and since she was doing this favour for him, she might as well do it to the best of her ability. What it cost him to put on a show with her in a starring role was no concern of hers.

'You look amazing,' Aristide proclaimed with satisfaction when he picked her up at the apartment.

Scarlett was still sucking her tummy in as she picked her careful way into the limousine in very high heels.

She wore a light jacket teamed with a silk camisole and flowing trousers. Her carefully straightened hair fell in a coppery tumble of smooth strands round her shoulders and her face was equally well made up. She had even had her nails done at a local beauty salon. Barely an inch of her was as nature had brought her into the world, she conceded ruefully.

Aristide feasted his attention on her. She glowed with her coppery hair swirling round her heart-shaped face, her cupid's bow mouth glistening, her eyes lit up like stars. As she settled, the jacket fell back on the camisole exposing the bountiful swell of her breasts and his attention lingered there, only slowly dropping to take in the rest of her. She looked ridiculously sexy without exposing any flesh. She had looked equally good the very first time he'd seen her with her curvy little body and shapely legs revealed by her close-fitting exercise gear.

Aristide was sheathed in faded designer jeans that fitted him like a glove and a shirt rolled up to his elbows, effortlessly elegant and far more casual than her in appearance, but then he didn't want her to look casual and potentially sloppy, she reminded herself wryly. He wanted the perfect, polished version of her that he had so rarely seen two years earlier because she had been too relaxed about being with him to spend hours agonising about her appearance and working on it.

She scrutinised him in a series of crafty little sidewise glances, not quite trusting herself to properly withstand the full spectacular effect of Aristide head-on. She looked and she expected to feel nothing because it had been so long since she had experienced any type of physical attraction. But little warm glimmers of awakening pulsed as she took in his bronzed profile, shifted down to a broad shoulder encased in cotton and to a sleek midriff rippling with muscle before lingering on a powerful masculine thigh and the potent swell at his crotch.

Reddening, she hastily glanced away again, registering in dismay that she was far too susceptible to even *look* at Aristide. It had been too long since she had been touched, held, driven mad with desire. Two years, not that long in the scheme of things, but two years in a sexless marriage had left its mark. She had shut down that part of herself that only Aristide had known, had just got on with her life, telling herself that she was more than happy with what she had established with Luke.

The atmosphere in the back of the limousine was tense and she slowly sucked in a breath, finally acknowledging how fiercely apprehensive she was of what lay ahead of her. When exactly was she planning to unveil her shocking truth to Aristide? Not at the party tomorrow, probably not before it either as she would have to take time getting dolled up for the event. Tonight? Where were they staying? Would there be other people there? She didn't want an audience if he lost his temper. After the party? What time would that be? Again, would they be alone? And they were flying home the next morning…

'You're very on edge,' Aristide scolded, closing a big hand over hers where she had braced it on the seat between them. 'I promise not to leave you alone with my mother.'

'I'm not scared of her!' Scarlett declared, fingers flexing in the light warm hold of his before pulling free as her head turned and inevitably her gaze met his. In all her life she had never been so conscious of another person's proximity.

Eyes as green as her party dress, startlingly bright against his bronzed skin, met her troubled scrutiny. Sudden heat curled up at the heart of her, little atoms of pure sexual awareness fizzing like live sparks through her bloodstream. Every tiny muscle in her body clenched tight and gooseflesh pebbled her arms below her jacket. Her mouth ran dry and her breath rattled in her lungs.

'Don't look at me like that…unless you want the consequences,' Aristide breathed with a ragged edge to his dark deep drawl.

Scarlett blinked rapidly and turned her head away, her whole body bubbling with nervous energy. 'I don't know—'

'I *do* know and so do you,' Aristide contradicted. 'But that's not why we're here together. I said platonic and I *meant* platonic but that also denotes that *both* of us have to respect the rules.'

Scarlett felt as if she were burning up inside her clothes and she stared straight ahead of her.

Aristide was rigid with self-control and hard as a steel girder. She had looked at him with longing and desire had leapt up in him so fast he was still gritting his teeth in a vain effort to control his libido. That *he* should have to remind *her* of the rules! He hadn't expected that little twist, hadn't been prepared for her to give him a look of that nature. Hungry, needy. And she couldn't hide it, was actually refusing to look back at him again while her cheeks were flushed as red as a traffic light.

'I suppose this was to be expected. Familiarity knocks us back into old behaviour patterns,' Aristide quipped much more lightly than he felt about the problem.

'Yes,' Scarlett squeezed out her agreement in a small tight voice. 'That's all it is.'

'So, let's move one step ahead and get our curiosity out of the way now,' Aristide suggested. 'One kiss and then we leave it there.'

Scarlett was so taken aback by that offer that she turned back to look at him in disbelief, sapphire-blue eyes wide and anxious.

'I bet we won't feel anything,' Aristide forecast with confidence.

Scarlett neglected to say that she had never been a

woman who bet on what struck her as a surefire loss but she understood what he meant and intended. If she felt nothing, she knew that it would be a huge relief.

'One kiss?' She checked the boundaries tautly.

'One should be enough to prevent us from ripping each other's clothes off before our flight,' Aristide mocked. 'And we need to work on your attitude to me before we float our pretence in front of an audience. You can't continue to pull away from me as though you're scared of me.'

'Of course I'm not scared of you!' Scarlett told him vehemently, even though she knew she was terrified of what he could make her *feel*.

'Good to know.' Aristide studied her with frowning force. 'I don't want to grab you but you're sitting a long way away.'

Scarlett swallowed with difficulty as he extended a lean hand to urge her closer. She grasped it and shifted along the back seat like a mouse told by a cat that she was not on the dinner menu but not really trusting the assurance.

Aristide curved long brown fingers to her cheekbone and tipped up her face. She collided with bright green eyes and it was as if an electrical charge shot through her veins. Quickly she closed her eyes and he lowered his head.

'Stop playing dead with me. It makes me feel like a lion hunting prey.' Taking his time, Aristide brought his mouth down on hers and slowly, smoothly tasted the parted promise of her lips.

She shivered, muscles snapping taut, every sense heightened as he drew her very slowly into his arms like a male determined not to spook her. She had almost forgotten what it felt like to be in his arms, but intense response raced up through her and, involuntarily, she pushed closer.

The scent of him washed over her, warm, male and achingly familiar even after all the time that had passed. Her body was frighteningly hungry for sensation and her lips parted in helpless invitation. He plucked at her full lower lip and ravished the moist interior of her mouth with his tongue. Her heartbeat hit earthquake mode, pounding inside her chest at such a speed that she was breathless. A tiny sound was wrenched from her.

The pressure of his lips grew more urgent and an explosion of fireworks flared and burst inside her, showering her with sparks and enveloping her in response. The feverish pulse between her thighs kicked up a heated notch. She wanted *more*, that fast she wanted *more* and it panicked her and drove her into instantaneous retreat as she broke away from him to surge back into her corner of the back seat.

'That was an enlightening experiment,' Aristide pronounced with finality. 'But we won't be repeating it any time soon.'

Inflamed by the aching pulse at his groin and angrily ignoring it, Aristide gritted his teeth in the humming silence and lifted the jewellery box beside him. 'I thought you might appreciate the return of this stuff for the occasion. Make use of it. Diamonds are acceptable at any time of day,' he informed her.

Grateful to have something to do with her hands, Scarlett clutched the box and flipped it open. Inside, in a careless tangle, lay every piece Aristide had ever given her. With a trembling hand she tugged the slender gold watch free and replaced her own. She couldn't believe that he had kept it all heaped in a box, almost as if he had gathered it up in one angry swoop and hidden it hastily away without making use of the jewellery boxes she had left in a drawer. Slowly, she teased the diamond and sapphire pendant out of the tangle. It had hurt to leave that glittering gem behind. He had given it to her the morning after their first night together in Dominica and she had loved it.

Aristide twitched it gently free of her grasp. 'Turn round,' he told her.

The coolness of the gold settled against her skin as he clasped it at her nape. Goosebumps broke out on her skin again and she shivered.

'Earrings,' he prompted.

She searched out and found the matching sapphire earrings and slowly attached them to her ears. 'The bracelet would be overkill,' she told him shakily.

'Up to you, but I would like to see you wearing most of it tomorrow evening,' he warned her.

With an absent fingertip she traced the exquisite diamond necklace still in the box. He had given it to her their one and only Christmas together and he had been annoyed when she'd taken it off to go home and enjoy Christmas lunch with her family instead of him, but he hadn't given her any warning that he would be spending the day with her. She couldn't possibly have worn a small fortune in diamonds and explained it to her parents' satisfaction.

She thought about that single wildly exciting kiss and burned with the guilt tugging painfully at her. She had fallen into that kiss and melted like ice cream on a hot grill. And he had known it too. Yet she *had* been happy with Luke, she reminded herself remorsefully. She had had so much in common with her best friend because they had shared the same outlook and similar interests. Luke had desperately wanted to be a father and he had been an amazing father for the brief months he had had with the twins.

Sadly, Rome and Alice wouldn't remember him helping with all those late-night feeds, soothing them when they cried by rocking them in his arms, tirelessly searching out toys that might catch their attention. Luke had adored Rome and Alice, and as a family they had flourished, would still have been flourishing had Luke's life been spared. She swallowed the lump in her throat and blinked back tears. Unfortunately, though, there had been a hollow at the heart of their relationship and both of them had had needs and dreams that the other could not fulfil.

In a daze of recollection, Scarlett boarded Aristide's private jet and sudden panic assailed her as she thought of the explanation that still lay ahead of her. She just wanted to get it over with, she acknowledged unhappily. She didn't want to try and pick some imagined perfect moment because truthfully there *was* no perfect moment in which to make such a revelation. But here they were trapped on a plane in privacy for a couple of hours. Didn't it make sense to come clean during the flight rather than risk being around other people when she told him?

'Have you become a nervous flyer?' Aristide enquired, watching her do up her belt on the other side of the opulent cabin with trembling hands, wondering why she had chosen not to sit beside him.

'Er...no,' Scarlett muttered unevenly. 'I just have something rather challenging to tell you and it's eating me alive with nerves.'

Aristide quirked an ebony brow. 'I can't imagine what that would be.'

He looked amused, emerald-green eyes alight with the hope that he was about to be entertained.

'It's not something you're likely to laugh about,' she warned him, more than ever intimidated by what she had to tell him because he was in no way prepared.

The jet roared down the runway and she breathed in slow and deep as it lifted up into the sky. In the si-

lence that followed, Aristide summoned the stewardess with the buzz of a call button. 'You need a stiff
drink,' he told her with a teasing grin.

As the stewardess retreated again, Scarlett released her seat belt and tried to relax with a glass of
wine gripped in one hand. 'I have two children...'
she began.

Aristide frowned, released his belt and plunged
upright wearing an expression of shock at her announcement that she was a mother. She had become
a parent with Walker? She had had a child with *him*?
That cut something deep in him that he didn't understand, and it hurt like the devil. He couldn't interpret
that distorted feeling of loss and betrayal and he took
refuge in outrage at the news.

'Two?' he questioned as that latter fact sank in.
'You were barely married a year before his accident!
How on earth could you have had two children in that
space of time?'

'They're twins,' Scarlett almost whispered, knowing that he had once had a twin brother, who had
passed away, but knowing little more detail beyond
that. 'They're eighteen months old, a little boy and a
little girl. They're *yours*.'

Aristide had frozen beside the built-in bar at the
front of the cabin, his big powerful body rigid with
savage tension. Unfortunately, it was as if a red mist
of incomprehension had suddenly come down over
him and captured him and he couldn't think straight

because he had no idea what she could feasibly be talking about. How could her children possibly be his?

'You were married to Luke Walker. If you had children, they can only be his. Why would you tell me that they're mine? Do you need money for some reason?' he prompted in a very detached voice.

'I'll just pretend I didn't hear you say that,' Scarlett said, flinching from that suspicion. 'I'm not in need of money, I assure you.'

'Why else would you suddenly tell me that you have kids and that they're mine?' Aristide demanded. 'This kind of discussion should be taking place in my lawyer's office, not directly with me. I don't deal with this kind of nonsense, not personally I don't,' he added.

'Whatever you choose will be fine with me,' Scarlett responded quietly. 'But I don't want any money and I'm not even asking you to have anything to do with the twins if you would prefer not to. I only spoke up because now that I've seen you again and so much has changed, it seemed time to tell you the truth.'

Aristide compressed his wide sensual mouth and dropped back into his seat, reaching automatically for his laptop. He still couldn't think straight but he was seething with a host of uneasy feelings that were deeply unfamiliar to him. The very thought of Scarlett having had children with Luke Walker made him feel vaguely nauseous. And she was acting out of character, which bewildered him. Scarlett had always been sensible. She was the last woman alive he would ever have thought would approach him with such an unlikely story. But it was crazy what people would do for money. He had learned that young. He had learned that being very wealthy merely made him a target just as it had made Daniele a cash cow for a greedy woman.

'I couldn't possibly have got you pregnant. I'm far too careful in that line,' Aristide informed her with startling abruptness.

'I was very careful too,' Scarlett countered defensively. 'It still happened. I don't know how. But it *did* happen and they *are* your children.'

'Who's listed on their birth certificate?' Aristide shot at her.

'I had to leave it blank.'

'There you are, then,' Aristide quipped very drily.

Silence filled the cabin as Aristide flipped through columns of numbers, barely able to focus on the screen while his brain worked busily in the background on the problem she had set before him. Denial roared through every inch of his lean, taut body. All he could think was that she had succumbed to temporary insanity or that she had financial problems and was hoping to make him step up now that she was on her own again.

But how could she try to con him when she knew that he would demand a DNA test as proof? Scarlett was intelligent and sensible, by no means a fool. Why would she do that? And even as he pondered that conundrum, another idea was burgeoning at the back of his brain.

Aristide stood up again. 'Are you telling me that there was a mistake?'

'A mistake?' she echoed tentatively.

'Because that makes sense. If you slept with both of us around the same time,' Aristide contended grittily, his lean, dark face hard as iron. 'Perhaps you conceived then and you assumed that *he* was responsible. That's why you left me and married *him*, isn't it?'

'No, it isn't!' Scarlett snapped back, shaken by the grubby picture he had fashioned of their past and the depth of his distrust.

'And then presumably when the children were born or some time afterwards, you and Luke realised that I had fathered them and *not* him,' Aristide suggested grimly. 'I have heard of such mistakes but I can't credit your claim in the first place because I always used contraception with you—'

'Oh, for goodness' sake, Aristide,' Scarlett groaned, appalled at the direction his inventive mind was now taking him in. 'Nobody but you could be the twins' father. Luke and I didn't have sex. He was gay. He married me because he was very keen to be a father and he thought he never would be. He married me when I was three months pregnant with your children!'

CHAPTER FOUR

ARISTIDE SHOT HER a look of scorching condemnation for all the false assumptions she had left him to make, both two years ago and in the present.

He was slowly absorbing what she had told him. On the outside he was now monitoring his every visible response but on the inside he was aware of a sensation that could only be described as intense relief... Luke Walker had been gay. Scarlett had *not* slept with him. Scarlett had *not* lied when she told him that her love for Luke was platonic. Together, those two facts were very important to Aristide. And last of all, if Luke couldn't be the father of her children, the chance that Aristide *was* the father now seemed rather more likely, even if he still couldn't grasp how Scarlett could have conceived on his watch. He was stunned into silence as the shock waves of all that information gradually trickled through him.

'You're shocked,' Scarlett conceded anxiously, rising out of her seat to approach the bar and seek out the white wine again for herself. 'I think I need another drink.'

Aristide watched her hold the bottle with a hand that still shook and he steadied it for her. He had never seen her drink even two glasses of wine in quick succession. She was shaken up, scared. Good, she should be, after what she had done and the indescribable mess she had created. And all without good reason, he reflected in stunned, angry disbelief. Why the hell hadn't she told him she was pregnant?

'Aristide...say something.'

'If your claim is correct, you and your husband literally *stole* my children from me!' he framed accusingly.

Scarlett looked up at him in stark dismay and hastily quaffed more wine in a nervous movement. 'It wasn't like that—'

'Do you have a photo of them?'

All of a sudden, Aristide was recalling the young children clinging to the older woman's legs when he had called at Scarlett's home.

Scarlett blinked in surprise and went back to her seat to grab up her capacious travel bag, rifling through the clutter to extract the small personal photo album she had brought with her, although she hadn't expected Aristide to ask to see a photo of the twins so quickly. Especially not directly after he had accused her and Luke of stealing his children from him. That accusation had cut like a knife when she had done everything within her power to protect him and her own family from the fallout of her accidental pregnancy.

Aristide took the album and began to flip through it. Image after image assailed his shrewd gaze and it grew a little glazed because he was viewing children overflowing with clear Angelico traits. Like him they had inherited the same wretched curls and naturally the little boy hadn't had a haircut yet because Scarlett had always hated it when Aristide got his curls cropped short. The little girl, on the other hand, was like a little curly-haired doll, much smaller than her brother. They were incredibly cute but he refused to say so.

'What are their names?' he asked instead.

'Rome and Alice.'

'Why Rome?'

Scarlett coloured and took another gulp of her wine. 'I worked out that that's where it must have happened…once the doctor told me the delivery date. It can only have been that weekend we spent there.'

'A vivid memory. I suppose I'm lucky you didn't call him Rhett or Ashley to follow family tradition.'

Her adoptive mother had been an enormous fan of the movie *Gone with the Wind* and christening her daughter Scarlett had probably been the most adventurous and colourful choice she had ever made in her life. But Nancy Pearson had waited until she was middle-aged to finally acquire a daughter and when that daughter finally came along, even her husband was unable to change her mind about what she chose to call her.

'Tell me why you did this,' Aristide murmured intently, suppressing his anger with every fibre of his being. 'I need to understand *why* you did such a wicked thing.'

Scarlett dealt him an anxious glance. 'It *wasn't* wicked.'

'But it was,' Aristide contradicted firmly. 'You didn't tell me. You didn't give me a choice.'

'But you didn't want children with me.'

Aristide gritted his even white teeth. 'What I wanted shouldn't have entered into the equation once you realised that you had conceived. We were a couple. Normal couples deal with such situations together.'

'We weren't a normal couple. You were away a lot of the time and there were other women in your life.'

Aristide stiffened. 'There *were* no other women.'

Scarlett dealt him a pained appraisal. 'Cosetta Ricci?'

'Cosetta is an old friend,' Aristide explained. 'She's a family friend, more than anything else.'

'But I didn't know that at the time!' she flared back at him in frustration. 'You were determined not to fully commit to our relationship and you were always reminding me that you planned to move on from me eventually—'

'That should have had no bearing on the discussion we should have had the minute you discovered that you were pregnant,' Aristide sliced in with ruthless bite. 'But we didn't have that discussion because you decided to keep your condition a secret from me.'

Scarlett lifted her chin in a defensive movement. 'I thought it was for the best all round. My father was dying of cancer and my mother was already distraught. I couldn't go home and tell them that I was about to become an unmarried mother. They would've fallen apart at the seams. They didn't deserve all that drama at that trying stage of their lives and they deserved better from me.'

Aristide had heard enough. Everyone but him had received due consideration. Luke had offered her a wedding ring and Scarlett had leapt at it to paper over the cracks and please her narrow-minded parents. Nobody had worried too much about how Aristide would feel or what he might want. Yet according to her that little boy and girl were *his* children, *his* blood, *his* responsibility. Rage settled like a heavy stone deep down inside him where he rigorously contained it.

As the silence smouldered, Scarlett began to speak again. 'I didn't want a termination or to part with my child to adoption. I knew you wouldn't want me to have them—'

Green eyes pierced her like steel knives. 'You knew *nothing*!'

'You said you didn't want children until you were middle-aged,' she reminded him doggedly.

Aristide's mouth took on a sardonic tilt. 'And like

every other human being on this planet, I adapt to changing circumstances when I have to.'

'I didn't want you to feel that you *had* to do anything for me!' she shot back truthfully.

'No, you were too busy being a coward to do the right thing and *talk* to me. There is no excuse for your lies of omission, no excuse for a woman who walked away from the father of her children and denied him his every legal right to marry another man,' Aristide completed tautly, and he sank back down into his seat, struggling to contain the fierce emotions washing through him in wave after sickening wave.

'Aristide…' Scarlett began uncertainly a few minutes later.

'I don't want to hear any more. To be frank, I've heard quite enough for the moment,' Aristide admitted flatly, seriously dissatisfied with the explanations he had received. 'But could you please transfer your wedding ring to another finger for the duration of the weekend? It will incite less comment. You can change it back once we leave.'

Scarlett looked down in dismay at her hand and swallowed hard. Even aware of a panicky need to placate Aristide in any way she could, she rebelled against the concept but, an hour later, she slid the ring off her finger and threaded it covertly onto her other hand. He was furious with her. He didn't understand what she had done or why she had done it. How could he?

Her parents had been elderly compared to his, raised in a generation with rigid moral and religious values. Aristide had never felt that he owed a debt to his parents as she had. Her home had been so loving and caring that she had always tried to be the best daughter she could be and the threat of breaking their hearts at an already challenging time in their lives had been more than she could bear.

Had she taken the easy way out? Had she been immature and foolish? But whatever Aristide might say now, he had *not* wanted children two years ago, he would have been highly suspicious of her falling pregnant and her conception would still have destroyed their relationship.

Photographers tried to ambush them at the airport in Florence but Aristide's security team headed them off. Shaken by the flash of the cameras and the level of interest in Aristide, Scarlett was belatedly very grateful to be dressed as the most polished version of herself as she climbed into the limousine that picked them up.

'Where are we going?' she asked stiffly.

'The family home where the party is being held. It's belonged to me since my grandfather died. He didn't like my parents much and he skipped their generation in his will,' Aristide told her wryly. 'That caused a lot of grief in the family circle, but then my home has always been a battlefield, so it was nothing new.'

Scarlett winced at that information. 'You must have been close to him.'

'Much closer than my parents were,' he conceded. 'But I could have done without the bad feeling incited by that will. My grandfather went through two nasty divorces that cost him most of his fortune, but the family properties like the one here and the one in London were held in trust and kept safe. After the second divorce, he spent his time travelling, so I didn't see much of him the last few years of his life.'

'That's sad.'

Aristide shrugged. 'It wasn't. He was happy. In the Angelico clan, happiness is not a given.'

'Why is it like that?' she asked, genuinely curious.

'Too many damaging events, too many bitter people. We have a complex history, but you and I have shared enough negative stuff for one day, so I won't get stuck into it right now, if you don't mind,' Aristide murmured, his strong profile clenching hard, green eyes cool as ice.

So, her children were a negative, Scarlett acknowledged with a sinking heart. But perhaps she wasn't being fair. He was right. She had not given him any choice. She had not spoken up when she should have done. She had not respected his rights as a father. Instead, she had grasped at the nice tidy solution she had seen in marrying her best friend.

'The twins are *not* a negative. I was referring to all the other stuff that goes with them...your silence, your marriage, the choices you made without consulting me,' Aristide specified curtly. 'That is all a very bitter pill to swallow.'

The car turned up a long steep driveway that carried them through deep woodland that slowly petered out into lawn. It was hauntingly beautiful.

'Is this the house?'

As the vast velvety stretch of lawns gave way to a gravel frontage, Scarlett stared wide-eyed at the building ahead, a vast stone property of ancient splendour such as she had never seen except in a history book. 'My word,' she whispered in consternation. 'It's a palace!'

'Palazzo Angelico. We're lucky the repairs have been completed in a timely manner. That's the main reason I suspect it was left to me. My parents let it go to rack and ruin—'

'But this *is* where you grew up,' Scarlett broke in, her wonder at such a childhood background patent and her curiosity on a high. 'Isn't it?'

'Daniele and I...yes. *Madonna santa!*' Aristide erupted without warning. 'It looks as though we're receiving a reception committee. What the hell are my parents doing here?'

'Perhaps something to do with the party?' Scarlett suggested weakly as she walked round the car to join him.

'They have their own home miles away,' Aristide said grittily, disconcerting her by closing a big hand over hers. 'Don't mention the twins, your marriage, anything. Anything you do and say can and will be held against you in their kind of company.'

'I wouldn't dream of it. Your mother paralyses my tongue,' she confided, but she was touched by his unexpected protectiveness.

'Cosetta is here as well. That's her car. Why is *she* here?' Aristide demanded wrathfully.

'Calm down. It's not important,' Scarlett murmured quietly as he urged her up a wide, shallow flight of steps into a huge echoing hall decorated with colourful frescoes.

Four people awaited them. One was clearly staff, standing a fair distance away. Another was an older man with grey hair, who bore a strong resemblance to Aristide. By his side stood an emaciated older but still very attractive brunette sporting giant pearls round her throat, a very smart dress and a bolero jacket. The third was a tall, leggy blonde, whom Scarlett also recognised from the magazine she had first seen her in, Cosetta Ricci.

Elisabetta's welcoming smile for her son fell off her face as though she had been slapped when she saw Scarlett. 'Aristide,' she purred in English, immediately turning to him as though Scarlett were invisible. 'We've moved in for the weekend and, of course, Cosetta, the darling that she is, has been helping me with the party planning. I must say the house is looking ravishing right now.'

'It must have cost you a king's ransom,' his father remarked with a faint air of disapproval.

'It's a shame you left it in such poor condition,' Aristide said drily.

'You look wonderful, Aristide…' Cosetta stepped forward to treat him to a continental kiss on both cheeks, which he tolerated but did not reciprocate. 'And *this* is…?'

It was the first time the little group had acknowledged her presence and Scarlett summoned up as warm a smile as she could manage. 'Scarlett Pearson—'

'Aristide's ex from years ago. How kind of her to step up for the occasion,' Elisabetta Angelico informed her husband, Riccardo.

'Scarlett is *not* my ex,' Aristide contradicted levelly. 'She's my special guest this weekend.'

In all, that welcome was a ghastly, awkward experience. Cosetta smiled continually but Scarlett was a woman too and she guessed that the blonde beauty had expected Aristide to walk through the door alone and be delighted by her presence. Spots of colour highlighted Cosetta's perfect cheekbones at his cool reaction. She did have better manners than Aristide's parents, however, because she made small talk until Aristide intervened to introduce Scarlett to the hovering male member of staff, who was called Andrea and managed the palazzo. Without further ado and with very few words more spoken to his silent parents, he guided Scarlett towards the grand marble staircase.

'My first mistake was agreeing to the party,' Aristide lamented in an undertone. 'Now I've got a home invasion to handle—'

'It's a *huge* house,' Scarlett pointed out gently, resting her hand on the carved balustrade of the stairs. 'Surely you need hardly see them? Your mother looked annoyed when you walked away so quickly.'

'It won't do her any harm,' Aristide bit out and then added, 'No, I don't mean that. Daniele begged me to be more forgiving in his last letter to me and I'm *trying*, but it's a challenge when my strongest memory of her is of her taking a belt to my little brother and calling him stupid because he was dyslexic.'

Scarlett was appalled. Unhappily she could picture Elisabetta being cruel because she had the superior assurance of someone who demanded high standards and punished those who failed her expectations. 'Maybe she's learnt better since then and regrets her treatment of him?' she suggested uncertainly.

Andrea spread open double doors on a big bedroom. Behind them, their luggage was brought up. As Aristide spoke to the man in Italian, Scarlett turned and noticed that all their luggage had been brought to the same room.

'Refreshments will be served out on the balcony,' Aristide breathed, striding across the room to throw open a door and disappear from view.

Scarlett followed him at a slower pace. He stood looking out over the gardens, his strong shoulders and back rigid with raw tension. The *home invasion*? He really didn't like his parents, and that image he had given her of his brother being beaten hadn't warmed her opinion either. As for his father almost sneering at him for repairing a property he and his wife had apparently failed to maintain while they lived there, Scarlett was no more impressed.

What she had to say now sounded terribly trivial in comparison to what she had witnessed. 'You didn't warn me that you were expecting me to share a room with you.'

Aristide swung round and raked impatient fingers through his curls. 'I wasn't expecting you to share with me but their presence in the house doesn't give me another option. We would look fake if we didn't share a room.'

Scarlett nodded agreement. 'I'll sleep on one of the sofas—'

'No, I will,' Aristide assured her apologetically.

Scarlett said nothing. He was far too tall to spend a night on one of those dainty sofas while she, being very much shorter, would manage fine and they did at least look well upholstered and comfortable.

The stone balcony with its shaded roof and ornamental facades was set up for comfort with padded seats and a table. She doffed her jacket and kicked off her shoes, determined to make the most of the sunshine and relax.

'I'm sorry about all the heavy-duty angst,' Aristide

framed, his lean, darkly handsome face taut. 'This wasn't how I planned to introduce you to my Italian home.'

'Let's face it, I put you in a bad mood before we even got off the plane.' Scarlett sighed. 'The reception committee was just the cherry on the cake.'

'I was planning to take you to my favourite restaurant in Florence for dinner this evening, but I suppose it would be rude to abandon my uninvited guests. Shall we be rude?' Aristide dealt her a hopeful look.

'No. You can take me there for lunch tomorrow instead. How would that be?'

Aristide frowned. 'Won't you be spending the afternoon getting ready for the party?'

Scarlett went pink and shook her head. 'I don't have an extensive beauty routine and I prefer to do my own hair.'

'You take everything in your stride like a trooper. Is that the teacher training coming out?' Aristide quipped as a maid in a tunic joined them with a laden tray.

Scarlett wrinkled her nose. 'It could be that I'm just lazy!'

He laughed, green eyes glittering in the sunshine. He had calmed down and she was relieved but still on edge. After all, he hadn't yet had the time to consider her unexpected announcement that he was a father and once that news settled in, how would he react? She dropped down into a comfy seat and poured the coffee. She wanted to ask more about Cosetta Ricci, who was clearly a great favourite with his mother, but she held her tongue because Aristide had had a trying enough day.

CHAPTER FIVE

SCARLETT DONNED A print cotton maxi and her sapphire pendant for dinner and emerged from the opulent marble-lined bathroom to see Aristide sheathed in a fashionable dark blue suit that looked amazing on him.

'You wore that dress in Dominica,' he recalled, studying her fixedly, picturing her shedding it on the sand and walking into the sea like a curvy little goddess who made his heart race and his blood run hot as lava.

'Yes, it's not designer,' she acknowledged ruefully. 'But I didn't come prepared for the number of social occasions that have suddenly cropped up ahead of us.' In fact, she was embarrassed that she had been so careful with what she had accepted in the weekend wardrobe. Aside from travelling outfits and the party dress, she had accepted only one other dress and it was short and unworthy of a dinner with his parents in a palazzo.

A slanting smile tilted Aristide's expressive mouth. 'It's still remarkably pretty.'

But Scarlett could tell by the rampant glow of his

emerald gaze that he wasn't really talking about the dress, more likely he was remembering her casting it off at his instigation and abandoning her inhibitions to swim naked on his villa's private beach. And no doubt he remembered even better what they had done once they had emerged from the water again. Her face burned but the clenching sensation in her lower body made her shift her feet uneasily, a tight hunger she was painfully aware of surging through her whenever he looked at her in that certain way.

Dinner was a grand event in the splendid dining room with a table large enough to seat two dozen people and the atmosphere was decidedly strained. Scarlett urged everyone else to speak in Italian and not mind her, which wasn't a problem for Elisabetta, who was studiously ignoring her even while Aristide drew Scarlett continually into the conversation.

Cosetta chatted to her, referring to exclusive places in London that Scarlett had never visited and sighing about the amount of travelling she did as a model while interposing the monologue with clever little questions about when Scarlett had first met Aristide, when they had reconciled and numerous other little asides. Scarlett ducked and swerved and held on to her privacy while Cosetta disclosed certain facts...

Aristide and Cosetta had always moved in the same exclusive social circle. Translation: you're out of your league.

Aristide didn't commit because his family had put

too much pressure on him to marry. Translation: you have no hope.

Aristide was exceptionally selective with women. Translation: the competition out there will slaughter you.

A sunny smile pinned to her taut lips as they climbed the magnificent staircase again, Scarlett was relieved that Aristide had excused them from the dinner table as soon as he saw the first yawn creep up on her.

'I have the impression that Cosetta was not quite to your taste.'

'She was trying in the politest way to learn my deepest secrets—of which she learned none—and frighten me off by intimidating me with your high standards. I think she believes that she would make you the perfect wife.'

'That's Cosetta. She has always been her own biggest fan,' Aristide said with amusement as they walked back into their bedroom.

Scarlett gathered up her silk pyjamas and went into the bathroom to change. When she reappeared, Aristide was stripping, not a shy bone in his magnificent body. She studied his lean strong back, the ripcord muscles rippling as he bent down in his boxer shorts, and forced herself not to stare like a sex-starved woman as she plumped up the sofa cushions and arranged her makeshift bedding before climbing in.

'I've been mulling over what you did to me all evening and I've reached certain conclusions. I ought to tell you what they are and clear the air,' Aristide startled her by confiding quietly.

'Okay,' Scarlett agreed nervously.

'I realised that if your husband hadn't died I would never ever have known that I have children.'

In consternation, Scarlett rolled over and almost dragged herself up into sitting position on the sofa. 'That's a dreadful thing to say!' she argued.

'But it's true. Luke *wanted* to be their father. A rich birth father in the wings who wanted to get to know his children would have been a threat because you didn't include me from the beginning. When were you planning to tell the children that he was *not* their father? The older they became, the harder that would have been and you would probably have avoided it,' Aristide contended, green eyes hard as iron on her troubled face.

Scarlett stared at him where he reclined, apparently fully relaxed against the headboard of the bed. He wore black PJ bottoms, nothing else. Bare-chested, he was a study of crow-black curls and polished bronze skin sheathing well-honed muscles in the softer light. 'I didn't avoid anything—'

'Well, you certainly were not active in informing me that I had become a parent. Did you consider contacting me in the months since Luke died? Did it occur to you that the twins no longer had a father of any kind and that there was space for me to be acknowledged?

My best guess is,' Aristide intoned levelly, 'that you were *never* going to tell me because that was the easiest thing to do. And don't say again that that's nonsense. If I hadn't attended the memorial service and followed that up with a visit, you would have had *no* immediate plans to tell me. Did the sight of me jog your conscience? Is that why I'm finally being informed that I'm a father?'

Scarlett was pale as milk, her blue eyes dark with strain. 'Finally? They're *only* eighteen months old, Aristide—'

'Eighteen months I've missed and can never recapture. Their birth, their first steps, first words,' he enumerated in a roughened undertone. 'What did I do to you to deserve that loss?'

Scarlett felt her tummy roll sickly and lay back down again on the sofa, no longer able to look at him. Remorse was roaring through her.

'I wasn't a drinker or an abuser and I was never unfaithful despite what you believed,' Aristide stated levelly. 'I didn't lie to you either. And yet you have behaved as if I wronged you terribly in some way.'

'You've said enough. I understand your feelings,' Scarlett mumbled wretchedly, hoping to bring the character assassination to an end. She didn't want to throw up his habit of dangling the threat of other women over her head. She didn't want to provoke an argument when both of them were already overwrought and she herself was exhausted.

'I had to speak up to have any hope of containing this anger,' Aristide confessed in a raw undertone. 'I trusted you until the day you sent me a text informing me that you were going to marry Luke. You have now betrayed that trust twice. With that sudden marriage *and* with the concealment of the twins.'

Her lips trembled, her eyes prickled, but she couldn't possibly cry with Aristide in the same room. He doused the light and she lay in the moonlight darkness staring emptily into the shadows while silent tears ran down her cheeks. She should have told him that she was pregnant right from the moment she found out and steeled herself against whatever his reaction might have been back then. Sadly, she had not been able to bring herself to break her parents' hearts.

And right now, she was learning something that she hadn't known about Aristide. He could control his temper, speak with clarity and hit every lethal target with accuracy and all without raising his voice in the slightest. He was so disciplined he had contrived to make light conversation over the dinner table with the parents he thoroughly disliked and he had not displayed a shred of the angry frustration that his most recent words had communicated to her. *You have now betrayed that trust.* That made her feel as though she had stuck a knife in his back the minute he'd turned away from her.

And was it true? Could it be true that there had never been another woman while she was with him?

Had their relationship been more stable than she appreciated? She could see now that she had subjected him to unfair treatment. She had panicked when she conceived. She had attempted to build herself up to the point where she told Aristide but she had failed time and time again and her insecurities had taken charge of her instead. As the weeks had passed, she had drowned in an ever-growing spiral of anxiety and then Luke had made his offer and it had seemed to her then that it was the perfect solution for a woman who wanted to keep her baby and a man who didn't want a baby. But, far too late to change anything, she was discovering that there was no such thing as perfect when it came to solving human dilemmas.

Aristide shifted position in the big bed. He knew she was crying. She hadn't made a sound, but he just knew it the same way he knew the sun would rise in the morning. He also knew that an intervention would be unwelcome. He wanted to grab her off the sofa and close his arms round her, but he knew she would lose her temper if he dared. But he had had to get it all off his chest before that anger flamed out of him in a much more damaging way.

Aristide was very practical. He didn't want to fight with Scarlett about decisions that could not be changed. He was well aware that if he wanted his children in his life, he had to accept the current situation with as much grace as possible. He had to move on, fix the damage and leave regrets and judgements in the rear mirror. What came next was more important than past mistakes.

Scarlett lay sleepless half the night, feverishly going over and over what Aristide had said. She began to see that she had made a crucial error right from the moment that she had realised she had conceived. It had not occurred to her that while Aristide might decide he no longer wanted *her* he might still want to be part of his child's life. She had tangled up their relationship with the baby she carried, not appreciating until now that they were two *separate* issues, two separate relationships, and that Aristide was quite entitled to break up with her and still be involved with his child. That was where she had gone wrong in her decisions, telling herself that she was choosing the best option for all of them, saving her pride sooner than face Aristide ditching her.

Her shoulder was lightly shaken. 'Breakfast is out on the balcony,' Aristide informed her.

Scarlett sat up with a start and discovered that she was now in the bed and alone, because Aristide was fully dressed and already disappearing outside again. She scrambled out of the bed in haste and pelted into the bathroom to splash her reddened eyes and clean her teeth before running a brush through her hair. Unless you were a vampire of myth, nobody looked good with red eyes, she decided ruefully. Back in the bedroom she put on the robe she had left on a chair and searched out the package she had dug out of her luggage and hidden on the floor of a dressing-room closet the night before.

She had to move on from the previous evening and all the horrible feelings that had surged up inside her after Aristide had admitted how he felt about what she had done. Somehow, she would make it up to him, she told herself ruefully, even if she didn't know how. She located her bag and took out the little photo album, swallowing hard as she gathered up her courage.

Aristide was talking in Italian on his phone when she joined him at the table. She set her birthday gift and the album down in front of him, watching an ebony brow arrow upward in surprise, and then she poured coffee for him and tea for herself. A selection of elaborate mouth-watering pastries and fruit was on offer and she helped herself because she was hungry, having been too stressed to eat much the night before.

Aristide put his phone down.

'How did I manage to end up in your bed?' she asked.

'You were tossing and turning at dawn and I lifted you in. You snuggled down and went straight into a sound sleep.'

Scarlett shrugged. 'Well, thanks. Happy birthday!' she added with determined brightness when clear green eyes collided with hers and she could feel her face burning up hot.

'Didn't you feel more like throwing it at me after last night?' he quipped lazily, relaxing back in his seat. 'Am I getting the album as well?'

'Yes. I should have told you that yesterday. I put it together for you,' she admitted stiffly, watching him flip through the photos again, pausing to treat some of them to a more thorough appraisal.

It was a beautiful day with a perfect blue sky and brilliant sunshine. She doffed the robe because she was too warm, all her attention locked helplessly to Aristide. Green eyes as translucent as sea glass, black lashes spiky and velvety dark, he was an incredibly beautiful guy and his hotness factor, she acknowledged, was off the scale. He smiled as he lifted her gift and began to unwrap it and she was grateful that she had thought to get him something because it was a much-needed ice breaker following that confrontation after dinner.

Aristide indicated the slim leather-bound copy of Andrew Marvell's poetry with a flashing smile of appreciation. 'This has to be the most thoughtful gift I will receive today and I'm grateful. I like to remember Daniele on our birthdays and reading some of these lines will bring him back just for a moment,' he confessed.

'How long has it been since…?'

'Six years. He took his own life, which was the

hardest fact for me to deal with because I tried to stay close enough to him to give him my support,' he admitted. 'He was an artist, very talented, very sensitive and bipolar, but he wouldn't take the medication that kept him on an even keel because he believed it stifled his creativity. He was already cut off from the family because he had dared to walk his own path. The artist's model he was crazy about cheated on him and he fell apart. He was in New York when it happened. I don't know that I *could* have changed his mind but at least I could have made the attempt if I'd been there.'

'Nobody's fault,' she whispered. 'Sorry, I didn't mean to rouse unhappy memories on today of all days. I just remembered out of the blue that you once said Andrew Marvell was his favourite poet—'

'You haven't roused bad memories. I make a point of remembering the good times on this particular day,' Aristide murmured smoothly. 'Now, tell me about Rome and Alice, what they like, what they don't like. I want you to flesh them out for me before I meet them.'

Relief spread through Scarlett, diluting her weighty sense of guilt. She went through the album with him and shared little stories until it was time for her to go and get dressed for their lunch out.

As she walked towards the bathroom, Aristide caught her hand in his. 'Thank you for not being defensive or moody or angry. Thank you for sharing the twins with me. We have to consider them and overcome our differences.'

Scarlett hovered, troubled eyes brightening as she met his intense green gaze. For an instant there was nothing inside her head but him and her whole body was warming at his proximity. She stretched up to try and kiss his cheek in an unstudied moment of affection but she couldn't reach him because he was far too tall. He laughed with rich appreciation, disconcerted by her approach but seemingly pleased at the same time. His hands settled on her hips and he lifted her up against him.

'Let me help, shorty,' he teased softly.

Predictably, Aristide did not aim at her cheek, he let his mouth drift gently across hers in an opening caress before crushing her parted lips under his with all the raw passion he had restrained when she had been in his arms the day before. Her head swam, her tummy flipped and her toes curled as he kissed her breathless. Excitement hummed low in her stomach and pinched her nipples into tight little buds. She closed her arms round his neck and kissed him back, revelling in the erotic flicker of his tongue delving and sliding against hers, enthralled by the tightness of his hold on her and the sensations engulfing her.

Aristide settled her down again on the rug below her bare feet. He skimmed her swollen mouth with the tip of a forefinger. 'Later,' he muttered thickly, his stunning eyes heavily lidded on a gleam of smouldering hunger.

In a daze, Scarlett walked into her bathroom and

shed her pyjamas. What was she doing? What was she inviting? Wasn't she muddying the waters of their platonic agreement? Why was she suddenly thinking that Luke had had his nights out during their marriage and had not been a faithful husband while she had stayed celibate? Luke had told her that she was free to do as she liked but Scarlett hadn't believed that she could cope with that sort of freedom within marriage. In any case, there had been no one else for her after Aristide, nobody she ever wanted or missed more than him.

She had been heartbroken when he went out of her life. Of course, she hadn't given him an option, had effectively staged her own exit by telling him that she was marrying Luke. She couldn't blame either Luke or Aristide for her poor choices. She had to stand up and be strong this time around with Aristide and, whatever happened, always tell him the truth. No more secrets or half-truths. And she wasn't about to make a fuss about a stupid kiss, was she? After Aristide had finally told her the story of his brother's death, they had both been in an emotional state of mind and they had got a little carried away, no big deal.

Elegant in a lavender shift dress of designer cut, Scarlett sat down at the beautifully furnished small table in the lush, leafy courtyard. Paper lanterns hung from the trees and glimmered in pretty colours in the sunshine.

Soft guitar music was playing very quietly somewhere in the background. 'It's really beautiful here.'

'It's incredibly exclusive and the food's amazing,' Aristide said as their drinks and menus arrived.

Scarlett sipped her wine and chose her meal, taking note of his suggestions. For the first time since she had left home, she felt relaxed, even though the party still lay ahead of her. So far, Aristide had reacted incredibly well to the revelation that he was a father and she was already looking forward to him meeting the twins, but she was also apprehensive about what the future might now hold. What would Aristide want from her? Shared custody or something more? Or even a lesser arrangement with only occasional visits? she ruminated worriedly.

Aristide removed something from his pocket and settled it down on the pristine white tablecloth. It was a small leather box adorned with the logo of a famous jeweller's.

Scarlett leant forward, tensing, her eyes enquiring. 'What is it?'

'Open it and see.'

She clicked open the lid on a magnificent diamond and sapphire ring. 'What's this for?'

'I want you to wear it this evening because I'm planning to announce our engagement.'

'Our...*what*?' Scarlett questioned in astonishment.

Aristide spread lean brown hands as if to soothe her. 'News of the twins is sure to make it into the media and I don't want you to be embarrassed in public. I'm aware that you work in a faith-based school. If we appear to be engaged and on track to getting married, it will lend us a respectable patina. For the present, it's a harmless pretence which will offer you protection.'

Aristide marvelled that he was speaking with such assurance, offering an engagement ring on a foundation of complete practicality when in truth he didn't know what he wanted to happen in the future. In fact, he was in turmoil. He was still angry and bemused by Scarlett's revelations *and* her behaviour but he already knew that he didn't want revenge and he didn't want to hurt her. In short, he wanted his children. He also wanted his children living with him but he had yet to work out how he could best achieve that ultimate aim. The ring created a link between him and the mother of his children and right then, it felt sufficient…as if he were protecting her and the twins by officially binding her and them to him.

Scarlett was stunned by the suggestion, still staring down at the gorgeous ring as though it might yet leap out of the case and bite her. 'But…but—'

'You know it makes sense. Those children are mine and I will be making all the legal moves necessary to have their birth certificates updated to reflect their true paternity. DNA tests will be required. It must be done,' Aristide insisted. 'There are inheritance interests to be considered. If anything were to happen to me tomorrow, I want to be confident that both you and the children are left financially secure.'

'Don't talk like that,' she urged, having lost colour. 'Not after what happened to Luke.'

Perspiration dampened her brow and she breathed in slowly and deeply to complain, 'You're throwing a lot at me without warning.'

'We're flying back to London tomorrow. I haven't got much time to work with,' Aristide pointed out levelly. 'Think it over. No matter what happens between us, I don't want anyone to think that I am ashamed of my children or of you. I'm not trying to trap you, *bella mia*, I'm trying to show you respect.'

And while he was showing her that respect, he reasoned grimly, he would be working on how best he could safely claim his children.

Scarlett's gaze dropped to the plate set in front of her. An array of tiny tasting dishes arrived next. She scooped up the ring box and placed it on her lap. Fake girlfriend to fake fiancée, it was a meteoric, speedy rise. And in reality, she was as stunned and breathless as if it were real rather than yet another pretence. He had laid it all out for her, nothing hidden, nothing that was really unexpected. It couldn't hurt Luke now if the twins' true paternity were to be legally established, nor did she have the right to deny her children their right to both the Angelico name and inheritance. And if the whole blasted, mortifying mess of her private life did contrive to make it into the tabloids, it would

surely be less embarrassing to have a ring on her finger, even if it were only a temporary detail. Below the
level of the table, she extracted the ring and slowly
eased it onto her engagement finger.

'Let's eat,' Aristide urged, smiling as the ring flashed
in the sunshine while she served herself.

'You do realise that your mother will be absolutely
raging about this,' she warned him in an undertone.

'It's my life, not hers.'

In something of a daze at the speed with which Aristide was changing the path of her life, Scarlett returned to the palazzo to get ready for the party. It was
only a fake engagement, she recollected, but it was
hard to look at that ring on her finger without remembering how it would have made her feel had he offered
her such a commitment two years earlier. Only he
hadn't, she reminded herself ruefully. It wasn't real,
nothing about their current status was real and it was
ridiculously sentimental for her to wish that Aristide
had offered her a genuine commitment. The time for
all that was long past.

The ground floor of the palazzo was busy, professional caterers interspersed with the household staff
hurrying in and out of doorways, emptying vans and
wheeling trolleys of equipment and china. Cosetta was
putting the finishing touches to a wonderful flower
arrangement, which Scarlett paused briefly to admire.

'That looks marvellous,' she said warmly.

Cosetta's eyes flickered. 'The florist created it. I'm only deciding where it will look best.'

Aristide's fingers flexed against her taut spine and Scarlett moved on towards the stairs. 'That was you being told that she considers flower arranging beneath her.'

An involuntary grin chased the tension from Scarlett's mouth. 'Oh, I know.'

'I'll see you later,' Aristide informed her, leaving her at the entrance to the bedroom they had shared the night before. 'I have business to discuss with my father. He runs our Italian office.'

Scarlett walked out to the balcony and scanned the fabulous view of the woods and the lawns and the glorious countryside in the distance. It was so beautiful that it felt almost unreal, rather like the fabulous diamond and sapphire ring adorning her finger. Settling down into a seat, she dug out her phone and rang her mother-in-law, Edith, to check on her children and share what had been happening since her arrival.

'Tom and I have been preparing for this to happen since Rome and Alice were born. Our only fear is that their father will want to exclude us from their lives,' the older woman confessed anxiously.

'I wouldn't allow that to happen. In any case, you're pretty much likely to be free of all competition in the grandparent field. I doubt if there will be much enthusiasm from Aristide's parents,' she admitted, having moved quietly back indoors lest she be overheard.

Aristide rapped on the bathroom door when she was putting the final touches to her make-up. 'Time to go down for dinner,' he warned her.

Straightening the straps on her beautiful gown, she walked out, registering that he must have got showered and dressed elsewhere, for there Aristide stood, poised, sleek and sophisticated in a tailored dinner jacket and narrow trousers, the lean dark beauty of his face spectacular.

'You look stunning,' Aristide commented with approval. 'I'll announce our engagement at dinner.'

'Isn't it a little too soon?' she pressed nervously.

'No, family members and close friends should be informed first.'

On this second evening the dining table was clearly going to be packed. Aristide threaded her through the chattering cliques, introducing her to aunts and uncles and cousins and one or two familiar faces she recalled from two years earlier. As she renewed her acquaintance with one of his friend's wives, she was asked where she had disappeared to back then and she laughed, reddened and bypassed the question, only then appreciating that Aristide had not shared the news of her marriage with anyone.

And then that same woman said, quite loudly, grasping Scarlett's hand and raising her fingers to the light, 'My word…is that an engagement ring? Does this mean what I think it means?'

As heads turned, Aristide smiled. 'Exactly what

it looks like, although we haven't set a wedding date yet,' he admitted, moving through guests to reach Scarlett's side and curving a supportive arm round her.

Mere feet away, Scarlett saw Elisabetta Angelico freeze, outraged dark eyes welding to Scarlett like stabbing icicles.

'I was planning to announce our engagement over dinner, but Christine's eagle eye beat me to it,' Aristide quipped. 'This is Scarlett, my future bride and already the mother of my children.'

Scarlett paled and tensed, unprepared for the second half of that announcement and the outcry of confusion that those words invoked.

'Yes, twins,' Aristide was soon explaining cheerfully, as though such news were mere commonplace. 'A little boy and a little girl, eighteen months old.'

A welter of congratulations followed. Scarlett was surrounded by women admiring the ring on her finger. They moved into the dining room for the meal and even by then talk had moved on to the subject of weddings and heaps of advice came her way. She pinched her thigh at one point to persuade herself that she was even figuring in such conversations, reminding herself that it was all fake and that no wedding was on the horizon for her and Aristide. Over coffee, she excused herself to go to the cloakroom and when she emerged, Cosetta awaited her, looking very much like the evil fairy attending a christening party in her sleek black gown with its plunging neckline.

'Surprise, surprise,' she murmured smoothly. 'You've played a long game with immense patience and now you think you're about to reap the benefits.'

'Do I?' Scarlett fielded, exasperated that the other woman was efficiently blocking her exit. She supposed, however, that Cosetta's ambition to marry Aristide had received a shocking dent and maybe she couldn't blame the beautiful blonde for such an attack.

'Aristide has you right where he wants you. He'll marry you and then claim custody of the children. That would be a win-win on his side. He divorces you, regains his freedom and no longer needs to consider a wife once he has gained the heirs this family needs.'

Scarlett shrugged a slight shoulder, wishing she did not still have to look up at the beautiful model in spite of wearing the highest heels she had ever worn. 'Aristide is a law unto himself. But I doubt very much that he would do anything likely to hurt his children. Don't worry about it. It's not your problem.'

'I was warning you for your own benefit!' the blonde snapped as she finally stepped away from the door.

'Mind your own business and I'll mind mine,' Scarlett advised in a mild undertone as she made her escape. She would pay no heed to Cosetta's doom-laden warning because Aristide had no plans to marry her.

Aristide was measured and cautious in most actions he took. He had stage-managed their entire relationship two years earlier, never ever promising what he had no intention of delivering. He had controlled and lowered her expectations of him with little occasional remarks that had always made it clear that he saw her as only a temporary amusement in his life. It was little wonder, she conceded then, that she had been riddled with insecurity when she was faced with telling him that she had conceived.

So, no, while he might not have lied to her or cheated on her, he *had* manipulated her by ensuring that she had little faith or trust in their relationship or its staying power. Only, she was now acknowledging, that latter truth did not excuse her silence about the existence of the twins. Indeed, it merely accentuated the reality that she should have told him she was pregnant instead of going to great lengths to hide the fact.

Guests were already arriving for the party. Aristide stood with his parents, smiling and laughing as though he had not a care in the world. For a moment she envied him that cool, calm facade and then she recalled his unhappy home life with his brother and the moment of envy ebbed away. Scarlett had been very much loved by her adoptive parents and had grown up in a happy stable home. While it was true that she had devoted a lot of attention to gratefully fashioning herself into exactly the daughter they had seemed to want and expect, she had never faced the kind of critical censure that was so clearly Aristide's experience with his parents. The senior Angelicos had wanted to hand-pick their surviving son's bride and Scarlett's reappearance and fertility had wrecked their ambitious plans and hopes.

As she walked over to join the group, Aristide immediately guided her away, doubtless protecting her from his mother's venomous gaze and waspish asides. He walked her down a short corridor into a magnificent ballroom, stowed her in a comfortable seat and signalled for drinks to be brought. Champagne was poured by a uniformed waiter, bubbles tickling her nose as she sipped. 'Why does your mother hate me so much?'

'Social status means everything to her. My father comes from a family that stretches back hundreds of years and was once titled. You don't have anything to boast about in your family tree and you are not rich. That's all Elisabetta cares about,' Aristide advanced grimly. 'She married my father for his superior social status and he married her because she's loaded. It was a suitable match made more by their families than by them. They don't even like each other.'

'What a depressing way to live. Well, no doubt they'll be very relieved when we split up again.'

'That's not quite the comfort you might think,' Aristide imparted. 'Your son and daughter will soon be my official heirs. Whatever happens in the future there is no way of getting around that fact. If it's any consolation, it's only my mother who is furious about our engagement. I don't think my father *cares* who I marry. We've never been close.'

The room began to fill up and the party got going. Aristide was hailed with birthday greetings and many gifts. Introductions were made over and over again. Scarlett's social smile began to make her facial muscles ache. They were constantly interrupted and her ring was repeatedly shown off and treated as though it were the eighth wonder of the world. Getting an engagement ring from Aristide Angelico appeared to be a feat of no mean order in the eyes of his guests. She knew what people were thinking: that he was marrying her because she had his children and for no other reason. It embarrassed her to be aware that that assumption was being made, even though it was the truth, and she scolded herself, telling herself that their pretend engagement would make their relationship look a bit more official, a bit more serious even when they eventually broke up.

'Did you ever see more young, beautiful women assembled in one place?' It was Christine Moretti speaking, the wife of an Italian industrialist with whom they had once dined out regularly in London.

Scarlett turned to the other woman with amusement and chuckled. 'No.'

'His mother has invited old flames of his and innumerable potential new flames to this party,' the brunette pointed out with a grin. 'You must be the most hated and envied woman in this room and you took him off the market *before* the party even started.'

'Not quite,' Scarlett parried, watching a ring of

gorgeous young women gathering round Aristide as he talked to a friend at the edge of the dance floor. 'It wasn't quite that simple.'

'Yes, but you were never one of the little yes-girls he used to date, and he was with you for a very long time in comparison to your predecessors. And then you simply vanished—'

'No. I married someone else,' Scarlett confided, knowing that Christine was trustworthy and her husband, Matteo, one of Aristide's closest friends and that that particular truth would be common knowledge sooner rather than later.

Christine's lips rounded into a circle of astonishment. 'Oh, so that's why—' And then she sealed her mouth closed again and grimaced. 'Sorry, I was about to be terribly indiscreet.'

Scarlett was mortified by her eagerness to know what her companion had almost revealed. But Christine switched the conversation to Rome and Alice and nothing more of a gossipy nature was voiced. *That's why what?* she wanted to gasp. *That's why what?*

The second surprise of the evening occurred a couple of hours later when she was crossing the room in search of Aristide, and his father, Riccardo, intercepted her and asked her to dance. Disconcerted by the invitation though she was, she accepted with a smile and contrived to move around the floor to an old-fashioned dance tune without stumbling over the older man's feet.

'My congratulations are a little overdue, for which I apologise,' he told her awkwardly. 'But I didn't want to risk causing a public scene with Elisabetta, who always expects me to take her side. Take it from one who knows, Aristide deserves a little happiness in this life and if you can make him happier, you have my vote and my support,' he told her with a warmth he had never shown in his wife's presence. 'I'm in London every month and I would love to meet your children.'

Taken aback by that speech, Scarlett sought out Aristide, extracting him with some difficulty from the group of glamorous women demanding his attention. 'You'll never guess,' she said then breathlessly. 'Your father asked me to dance and made a lovely speech. He's totally different away from your mother.'

Aristide frowned. 'I can't imagine that.'

'I think he's scared of her,' she whispered. 'But I'm sure you know more about that than I do.'

'I've had very little to do with him,' Aristide admitted. 'When I was growing up, he was always at the office or I was at school. If he was pleasant to you, I appreciate it, but it's still a case of too little, too late...'

'I suppose so,' Scarlett sighed, realising that she was scarcely entitled to an opinion on the strength of one friendly approach from the older man. Dropping the awkward subject, she moved closer and said, because a DJ had just taken over and the first energising beats of a tune were sounding out, 'We could dance...'

Aristide groaned. 'You know I don't dance.'

'Just stand there. I'll dance round you,' she teased. 'That's one of my favourite songs.'

Aristide stayed on the edge of the floor watching her lose herself in the music, fluid hands swirling, feet moving to the beat. The fabric of her dress drifted against her shapely body and then flipped back to outline the firm swell of her full breasts and the bodacious curves of her feminine hips. He was mesmerised by her. A surge of lust roared up inside him with hurricane-force efficiency and he went hard as a rock in response.

Stalking forward, he reached for her and tugged her into the circle of his arms. '*Be* with me tonight,' he urged in a raw, hungry undertone.

CHAPTER SIX

ARISTIDE SENT SCARLETT a winging glance from scorching green eyes and her tummy flipped and her mouth ran dry but she knew she wasn't going to say no the same way that she knew she needed to breathe. She felt alive again, she felt wanted, *needed.* Intelligence was telling her not to make too much of the attraction that had always flared between them, but her body and her heart were singing an entirely different tune because this was Aristide and he made her feel stuff no other man had ever matched. In an atmospheric silence, he walked her out of the ballroom, which was already thinning of company as midnight was long behind them, and directed her upstairs.

Scarlett walked over to the dressing table and began to reach up for the clasp of the diamond necklace.

'Allow me,' Aristide murmured, his silhouette tall and strong and dark in the mirror behind her.

The silence smouldered. She trembled as cool fingers brushed her nape and he leant forward to place the glittering necklace down. The scent of him, warm and male with only a hint of cologne, flared her nostrils, the aching familiarity sending her back in time. His lean brown hands dropped down to lightly rest on her narrow shoulders.

'Is this a yes or a maybe…or a no?' he asked sibilantly.

'Yes,' she pronounced shakily, terrified in one way of what she was doing, wildly exhilarated in another.

He ran down the zip on the dress, tipped the shoestring straps down and let it fall to her feet. She was so on edge, so worked up before he could even touch her that she almost gasped. She stood there frozen in her very high heels and the flimsy lace strapless bra and beribboned panties she had selected to wear with the dress.

'*Madonna mia*…don't wake me up. I've died and gone to heaven,' Aristide groaned in a roughened undertone.

'I didn't have the right bra to go with this dress. It's not for you,' she gabbled, defending herself against the suspicion that she could have dressed up in the lingerie just to tempt him. 'I thought we were going to be in separate rooms—'

He entwined her fingers with his and guided her over to the carved ottoman at the foot of the big bed. He stationed her between his lean powerful thighs.

'What are you doing?' she gasped.

'I'm savouring you like a fine wine,' Aristide told her, pistachio-green eyes roaming over the proud swell of her breasts, which segued down to her shapely waist and full feminine hips. Breathing in deep, he shrugged off his jacket. 'You look extravagantly gorgeous. Like a mirage—'

'What's got into you?' Scarlett demanded, losing patience. 'I don't like standing here like an artist's model. My body's not the same any more. I've got stretch marks and a C-section scar. I'm nobody's gorgeous mirage—'

'Nobody's but mine,' Aristide growled, levering her down into his lap, pausing to slip off the ridiculously high heels as he kicked off his own shoes, peeled off his socks, gathered her close. 'C-section?'

'Last-minute emergency. The cord had caught around Alice's neck—'

Aristide paled. 'Was Walker with you?'

'Not until afterwards. Edith, his mum, was there. Luke was interning at an office miles away that day. The twins came early. Edith was better than he would have been anyway because the surgery would have freaked Luke out. He was very squeamish.'

'I would have coped,' Aristide proclaimed with pride. 'And I should've been there when my daughter's life was at risk—'

'We were lucky. It was a very good maternity unit.'

'I should've been there,' he said again with regret.

Scarlett framed his high cheekbones with her hands to distract him from that sensitive subject and teased her lips along the edge of his.

Aristide took the invitation with alacrity, driving

her soft lips apart in a ravishing, possessive kiss and then standing up with her still held in his arms. He brought her down on the bed and stood over her, ripping off his shirt, unzipping his trousers. As he came to her, Scarlett ran her finger down the intriguing little line of dark hair bisecting his flat stomach and he shuddered with gratifying responsiveness.

'Not likely to last long this first time,' he said raggedly, coming down to her with one driving kiss.

Scarlett speared her fingers into his curls to break the kiss and collided with glittering emerald-green eyes, her own anxious. 'You need to protect me. I'm not on the pill any more.'

Aristide stalked into the dressing room. Doors slammed open and shut. He reappeared and slung a handful of foil packets on the bedside cabinet. She looked at him as he came back down to her again, scanning the lean powerful musculature of his torso, the tautness of the muscles rippling with every movement and the awesome outline of the erection the boxers couldn't hide. He gave her a sudden flashing grin. 'See anything you like?'

Her face was hot but Scarlett merely inched a slight shoulder up in a shrug. 'Maybe,' she said.

'You want me as much as I want you…don't you?' he prompted, all of a sudden less confident than he had seemed earlier.

'Yes.'

It was a whisper because once she had made serious

decisions about intimacy with him, but they were not in that familiar place any more. What they had now had no safe boundaries. She was running a risk and she knew it, but she didn't want to think too deeply about it, lest her pride and her common sense force her to go into retreat. No, this way, this way, she thought ruefully, was easier. She wanted Aristide more than she had ever wanted him in her life and she had not the smallest wish to miss out on an opportunity that surely wouldn't come again.

He ran sure hands up over her hips and waist to release her bra. The cups fell away from the lush mounds, and he buried his face there for several seconds. 'I love the scent and taste of your skin.'

His lips engulfed a prominent pink nipple and her breath caught in her throat. Even as an arrow of heat darted down into her pelvis and made her squirm, memories were making it a challenge for her to stay solidly in the present. She remembered Aristide once returning to her after a few days' absence and ambushing her in the hall of his penthouse apartment, so impatient to be with her again that he took her against the wall, hard and fast. Now, as he teased at her sensitive buds and shaped the swell of her breasts, she was light-headed with the flood of sensation assailing her, awakening her body again after what felt like a long winter.

He traced the heat and dampness at the heart of her and excitement raced through her in an intoxicating surge. When he followed up by shimmying down her body to tease the most tender and responsive bud of all, her body went liquid and then shot up the scale to the sharp feverish edge of desire. She lifted her hips, twisted and arched her back while he toyed with her, knowing exactly what drove her crazy and providing it. The pulsing ache of desire controlling her rose to a high she could not contain, and she went soaring with a cry into a concentrated climax that made her flop back against the pillows like a boneless doll.

Aristide skimmed off his boxers and ripped open a condom packet with his teeth.

'Risky,' Scarlett told him, twitching it from his fingers and sitting up to smooth the contraceptive down his boldly virile shaft with a fierce determination, born out of a need not to run the smallest risk of another accidental pregnancy. After all, the likelihood was that the twins had been conceived because one of them had been careless without even realising it.

Aristide was taken aback by that gesture. It was the first time she had done that with him. Was he a fool to have simply assumed that she had been faithful to a husband who had had no sexual interest in her? How did he know that there had not been other men? Well, that move had filled him with suspicion. That instant of disquiet, however, didn't lessen his fierce arousal one jot.

Why was he even thinking of something so trivial? Emptying his mind of such disturbing, confusing thoughts, Aristide shifted over her, lithe as the superbly fit male he was. She closed her arms round his neck and knocked him back in time to the night he had called her a spider monkey for the way she wrapped herself round him in bed. He washed out that thought for being inappropriate. All of a sudden, he was on his guard again, awash with lust, but now wary and striving to be cautious. Pushing her thighs back, he sank into the hot, tight welcome of her with a sound of deep masculine pleasure. And then there were no more thoughts, not a single one.

Still floating on a sea of endorphins, Scarlett moaned as his fast penetration stretched her tight channel and he drove deep. An eddy of blissful sensation spread through her lower body and she gave herself up to the enjoyment, rising up against him as he plunged into her, the ferocious beat of hunger pounding through her as fast as her racing heartbeat and pulses. Excitement seethed like a cauldron inside her and the knot of tension building within again rose to an agonising peak. A split second later, she convulsed under him as he vented a groan of harsh masculine satisfaction and she writhed, caught up in the same frenzy of excitement until the throbbing waves of sweet pleasure washed through her sated body and left her limp.

'Even hotter than I remember,' Aristide said raggedly, springing off the bed to stride into the bathroom. 'Do you want a bath?'

'Yes.'

A little spooked by the speed with which he had vacated the bed, Scarlett was still searching for her wits. Recalling that she hadn't even taken her make-up off, she scrambled out of bed and snatched up her robe, tying the sash with shaking hands. Had she done the wrong thing? Had she made a fool of herself when she fell back into bed with him? How would that renewed intimacy affect their already complicated relationship? She suppressed a sigh, knowing it was too late for regrets.

While the bath filled, she took off her make-up and removed the rest of her jewellery. Aristide was in the shower and the sight of his tall, bronzed body through the misted glass took her back in time again. *Stop that*, she told herself. *Wise up, this is now and everything's changed...everything's different...although not the sex.*

She had missed Aristide. She had missed their physical connection as well. Was that all this had been? A sentimental walk down memory lane? She doffed the robe, studied the wildflowers floating on the surface of the water and the scent of aromatic steam rising. He had always prepared baths like that for her and once she had thought it was so romantic, when he automatically bought luxury bath treatments for her. Had he readied the bath for her this time without even thinking? Or was he making some sort of point?

She sank into the water with a sigh of appreciation. A hug would have meant more to her than the bath though, she reflected ruefully.

Aristide emerged from the shower and towelled himself dry, wrapping a dry towel round his narrow waist and lingering.

'You put the contraceptive on for me…you never did that before,' he remarked abruptly.

Already flushed from the heat of the bath, Scarlett was mortified. 'No, it was my first time, but you seemed…careless with it. Hasn't it occurred to you that I'm terrified of getting pregnant now?'

Aristide nodded slowly and the brooding expression on his lean, dark features cleared and the stiffness dropped from the set of his broad shoulders.

'I spent weeks and weeks trying to work up the courage to tell you I was pregnant,' she reminded him.

'And why didn't you?'

Scarlett hugged her knees and rolled her eyes simultaneously. 'It wasn't that simple. I thought you'd blame me. I thought you'd want me to have a termination and I didn't want one. It's all very well talking about an unplanned pregnancy civilly but you're talking now with hindsight and the one thing I did know at the time was that you definitely didn't *want* a baby!'

Aristide elevated an ebony brow. 'Did you?'

'Not at first but I warmed to the idea after the first

ultrasound. They became real little people to me very early on and I just loved them instantly,' she confided softly.

Aristide stretched down a hand. 'Come on, it's very late…back to bed.'

Scarlett smiled up at him, sunny, natural. Aristide tensed and then she grasped his fingers, and he hauled her bodily from the water. He enveloped her in a towel as she complained about the water streaming everywhere, and patted her dry.

He lifted her naked and threw back the bedding to settle her down again.

Leaning over her, he stroked a strand of hair out of her eyes. It was messy and tousled because she had put it in a bun for her bath and let it down again. For the first time since he had seen her again, she seemed relaxed. His mouth drifted down on hers in search of her sweetness, her unique taste, the caress travelling down her slender neck to linger at her pulse points and suck on the sensitive skin.

'Don't you dare give me a love bite,' she said, breathless in the wake of that erotic onslaught. 'We're not teenagers.'

'I'm feeling as randy as one, *bella mia*,' Aristide confided with a slashing grin, shifting against her to acquaint her with his erection.

She rolled against him, fingers splaying across his chest, eyes closing, lips curving up as he carried her hand downward to encourage further exploration.

'My blood's running too hot for this,' he said raggedly only minutes later, reaching for contraception before lifting her bodily onto her knees and thrusting deep.

Scarlett gasped, her excitement on the rise again, and what followed kept that excitement at a sustained high for long, breathless, sweaty minutes. Surging over the peak of pleasure again, she collapsed, boneless.

'I'm never going to move again.'

'Is that a challenge?'

Her eyes were drifting closed as she closed an arm round him. Minutes later, she was fast asleep.

Aristide, in comparison, emerged from that surfeit of pleasure with a sense of shock. He knew that he hadn't enjoyed himself to that extent for years, but he also knew that he was fishing in dangerous waters. He didn't want to slide into a rerun of that past relationship with Scarlett, did he? No, of course he didn't, he assured himself squarely. He dared not trust her. They were already stuck in a fake engagement for the foreseeable future. It could get messy, *very* messy considering that she was the mother of his children. He had allowed his libido to overrule his good sense. He would have to make it quite clear where they both stood in the morning.

Scarlett woke to breakfast in bed.

She was embarrassed as the maid furnished her

with a lap tray. She had slept in. Aristide had kept her awake half the night and as usual had risen with the dawn, unaffected by his own athletic performance between the sheets. As she pulled herself up against the pillows, carefully keeping the sheet raised to conceal the fact that she was naked, she noticed that their cases were lying open in the dressing room and being filled by another maid.

At the point where she was wondering where Aristide was, he strolled in from the balcony, a cup of coffee cradled in one lean hand. 'Sleep well?' he asked lazily.

Although he was smiling she could feel the tension in him and she wondered why he was trying to hide it. 'Like the dead. Could you throw me my robe?' she asked.

Setting the lap tray aside, she dug her arms into the sleeves of the robe and wrapped it around her before leaving the bed to head into the bathroom and freshen up. If there was one thing guaranteed to make a woman uncomfortable it was being forced to greet Aristide, fully clothed in an elegant suit, shaved and immaculate, when she hadn't even had the chance to brush her hair. She packed up her toiletries at speed and dropped them into the case being packed for her before extracting her outfit for flying home and setting it aside.

'How long do I have before we leave?'

'An hour,' he told her.

'You should have wakened me earlier.'

Scarlett was hungry. If she hadn't been she would have pushed the tray away and got dressed. She ate her pastry, cut an apple into segments and drained her milky coffee while Aristide moved restively around the big room. Setting the tray down, she went to get dressed, emerging fifteen minutes later in a sundress with her make-up done.

'You suit dresses—'

'Aristide, just tell me what you're here to tell me,' Scarlett sliced in. 'Or save it for the flight.'

'Am I being that obvious?'

Scarlett released her breath in a soft hiss. 'Pretty much. If it's about last night, keep it to yourself.'

His brows drew together, his lean, darkly handsome profile taut. 'I've got us both into this no-man's-land. I should be the one to steer us out of it again.'

'Well, start steering,' Scarlett advised curtly, walking into the bathroom to pack her cosmetics and grab her brush, dropping them into the case for the maid and gently closing the door on her presence.

'Put your engagement ring on,' Aristide reminded her.

Scarlett rammed the sapphire and diamond ring back onto her finger and added the rest of her jewellery more slowly. 'I know this is all fake,' she reminded him. 'I'm not expecting anything more from you.'

'Last night was ill-advised—'

'Wonderful how it took you all those hours before

the dawn to reach that conclusion,' Scarlett sniped helplessly, so hurt and so angry she wanted to strangle him.

In the interim the dressing-room door opened and their luggage was wheeled out, the bedroom door finally flipping shut while the silence between her and Aristide stretched longer and drier than the Gobi Desert.

'You're annoyed with me.'

Scarlett spun to look at him, her dark blue eyes very bright. 'Was it revenge?'

'What on earth are you talking about?'

'Sexual one-upmanship. Let's face it, you're much angrier with me for staying quiet about the twins than I am angry with you,' Scarlett stated.

'It's not like that. I'm not that petty,' Aristide proclaimed with distaste. 'But this has been a roller coaster of a weekend from the moment you informed me that I was a father. I haven't been myself. When I suppress things, the tension only rises. Sex is a terrific release for tension.'

Scarlett walked into the bathroom, filled a glass of tap water and walked back out again to fling the contents at him. She didn't even have to think about doing it. Hitting back was automatic.

'*Porca miseria!*' Water sprinkling his face and soaking his shirtfront, Aristide stared back at her in a shock that would have been comical in any other circumstances.

'And I'm not going to apologise,' Scarlett declared

defensively. 'Because that's the least that you deserve. Don't tell me that you used my body to get rid of your tension unless you're prepared to take the consequences. When you get cold feet, just call it cold feet. An explanation is unnecessary. We got carried away. It was a one-night walk down memory lane. It's never likely to happen again. Can we please forget about it now?'

Pale beneath his bronzed complexion, Aristide stalked into the dressing room to change his shirt. When he reappeared, he said, 'I want to go straight from the airport to meet the children. Please organise that.'

She remained rigid, her flushed face expressionless. 'I'll tell my in-laws.'

'What do they have to do with it?'

Scarlett flashed him a look of reproach. 'Who do you think has been caring for them while I'm away? Edith and Tom are very attached to the twins.'

Aristide's lips compressed and he said nothing more. Indeed, neither of them exchanged another word during the drive to the airport. Buckled into her seat on the jet, Scarlett lifted a fashion magazine and stared numbly down at it. She was devastated and she knew it, but she didn't need to advertise the fact. The huge pain, the emotional wound of his rejection, threatened to pull her into a black hole of despondency but she resisted it like a soldier on the front line. Aristide had hurt her before with stray phrases—Shakespeare he was not and would never be. He was more like a machine gun spitting out unstoppable fire. She would deal with the hurt *later* and in the meantime she would be the soldier doing her duty.

Everything between them had changed. The past was dead and gone. Aristide was currently back in her life in a totally different guise as the twins' father. She would have to cope with that without getting emotional or reliving what he had once meant to her. She didn't have a relationship with him any more, but he *would* have an ongoing relationship with her children. Welcome to learning the art of being civil, she thought facetiously. How could she be polite and distant with him when she now hated him?

Scarlett assumed that she would learn, and probably the hard way since that seemed to be the way she learned most things with Aristide Angelico. She hated him but she hated herself more for being so foolish, for ditching her pride and sense of self-preservation in return for intimacy with the man whom she had once loved. What else had it been? Aristide would never allow it to be anything more than sex with her. She was the ex; she belonged in his past and not in his present.

So, why was she *so* hurt? Aristide was not a forgiving sort of person. He would never forget that she had once married another man and hidden his children from him. Whichever way she looked at the situation, she had wronged him. Why was that reality so clear to her now when she had not seen it two years ago? But she knew why. She had panicked. She had chosen ditching Aristide and running away into a safe marriage with Luke over simply telling the truth. And Aristide despised her for that choice. Could she really blame him?

Scarlett did, however, blame him for the night that had just passed, for the intimate ache of her body and the use he had coldly, cruelly made of it. He had ripped away the pretence that she could *ever* be indifferent to him. Now, here she was, shattered into so many broken pieces. She had acted like the most stupid fool, and she had stirred up feelings again, feelings that belonged only in the past. Her damage was self-inflicted, and she wasn't allowed to start feeling sorry for herself. Last night, Aristide had given her plenty of opportunities to back off and say no. He hadn't lied to her. He hadn't seduced her. He hadn't made any smooth promises. If it had been an act of revenge on his part, he certainly hadn't shown any form of satisfaction at the end result.

And the end result for her, anyway, was turmoil. Turmoil she did not need to be experiencing on the brink of letting Aristide meet his children for the first time. Nothing could change what had happened between them. She already regretted throwing that glass of water at him. She shouldn't have shown him how upset she was, shouldn't have put her *hurt* on display like that…

CHAPTER SEVEN

SCARLETT LEANT ACROSS the aisle to settle the engagement ring down on top of Aristide's laptop as the jet taxied back into the airport in London.

'You agreed and you need to keep up that pretence for your sake and for the children's sake,' Aristide intoned grimly, while he wondered how he had contrived to mess up their present relationship quite so spectacularly. 'We won't gain anything from you taking the ring off—'

'There is no "we",' Scarlett riposted.

Aristide gritted his even white teeth, despising the drama he had unleashed with every fibre of his usually disciplined being. He tossed the ring back to her with studied casualness. 'You wear the ring for the present. It makes sense. You know it does. The public at large prefer romance and reconciliation to a former couple who are bitter enemies engaging in a custody battle.'

As Scarlett lifted the ring again before it could roll onto the floor, she froze into icy dread. *Custody battle?* Was that first mention of legal action a throwaway threat offered in the heat of the moment? Or a taste of what lay in her future? Whatever, the mere suggestion that he could fight her for custody of her children chilled her to the marrow. Reluctantly compliant, she thrust the sapphire and diamond ring back onto her finger, willing to admit that she had tossed it back at him in a rather juvenile gesture.

He brought out a side of her she seriously disliked. She compressed her lips over that continuing self-denigration. Beating herself up for her mistakes would do her no favours. At the end of the day, she could not escape Aristide's determination to become a part of the twins' life. What she had yet to learn was how to handle that development with grace and style. It was all the personal ramifications of further exposure to Aristide that were causing her grief. She was too sensitive and emotional about Aristide and that did have to change because she was the only one of them likely to be hurt by any fallout.

Aristide reappeared from the rear cabin, more casually clad in jeans and a long-sleeved green tee. 'I assume that this is more suitable clothing for meeting young children,' he said, skimming an almost self-conscious hand off a lean, taut, denim-clad hip.

Aristide was nervous, she recognised in surprise. 'How much do you know about toddlers?'

'Next to nothing. There are young kids in the wider family circle but none that I've had anything to do with. Only a few of my friends have children and, again, I've had little personal contact with them.'

'Rome and Alice are very sociable. I shouldn't think you'll have much of a problem getting acquainted,' she told him soothingly, aware that it would be easier for all of them if the first meeting went well.

Aristide studied Scarlett covertly when the limo got stuck in traffic. He hated the silence, the absence of her sunny smile and her chatter. But he had done what had to be done, he told himself squarely. He had redrawn the boundaries between them. *Again?* He flinched from that sarcastic inner voice. So, he had a weak spot when it came to sticking to business with Scarlett. He would deal with it and move on, get back to his life, full closure achieved, wouldn't he? How soon, though, would he manage to stop craving her like some toxic, mind-bending drug?

She was dangerous. She knocked him off balance, came between him and his wits. But he had too much pride to be sucked in by her again. He couldn't trust her, he *knew* that he couldn't trust her. She was seriously bad news for him, so why was it such a challenge to keep his distance?

It was true that once she had made him incredibly happy, but the aftermath of that experience had proved to be a punishing, horrible challenge. He wasn't going to put himself through hell and rejection again. From now on, he would respect boundaries and it would benefit both of them. *Accidenti!* So, why was he still looking at her and thinking about her?

Sooner than Scarlett had deemed possible they arrived at the apartment she had once shared with Luke. In the midst of reacquainting Aristide properly with Edith and Tom, she was swarmed by Rome and Alice and almost unbalanced by their enthusiastic welcome home. Laughing, eyes damp with guilty tears for having left them in the first place, she stumbled into the living room and got down on the floor with them, abandoning Aristide to his first meeting with her in-laws.

'Edith and I will bow out now and leave you in peace,' Tom said from the doorway, as always a sensitive, discreet man.

Scarlett rose to give him an impulsive hug of gratitude, knowing that the older couple were the parents she would have chosen for herself, had there been a choice, because they were so much more open, liberal and young in outlook than her adoptive parents had been.

Aristide sank down on the leather sectional and Alice surged over to him instantaneously to lean up against his knee.

'She likes men,' Scarlett muttered awkwardly, watching Rome hover warily beside his building blocks as if he were awaiting some kind of threatening move from Aristide.

'She must miss Luke.'

'They were only babies when the accident happened. I doubt if they remember him now.'

Alice clambered up on the seat with Aristide, stuck her thumb in her mouth and steadied herself on his shoulder.

Almost mesmerised by her proximity, Aristide studied her vivid little face and her huge smile when he smiled at her. 'She's ridiculously pretty.'

Not to be outdone by his twin, Rome climbed onto the seat too and then climbed over Aristide as if he were a mere obstacle in his path.

'Rome will be more of a challenge,' Aristide guessed, lifting Alice down onto the floor and advancing on the building blocks to pile them up into a tower.

Rome smashed them down and chuckled with delight.

'We could take them into the garden so that they can play...or to the playground at the park,' Scarlett suggested, trying to be helpful as Rome raced about the room with a toy aeroplane making loud noises. 'They're very active for a very short time and then they need a nap.'

'Playground,' Aristide selected. 'We'll be alone there.'

'We are alone here. Edith and Tom won't interfere,' Scarlett said mildly.

Scarlett tried to understand as she packed a bag for the playground to cover all toddler necessities. This was Luke's former home, photos of her late husband and of her with him and the twins everywhere, and if Aristide didn't feel comfortable here, she should make allowances, she reasoned ruefully. What she had not expected in the outing was Aristide's security team wanting to scout the location first and taking watching stances to observe from the tree line.

Luckily, it was late afternoon, and the park was mostly deserted. The twins swarmed over the infant slide with the interest of regular visitors, quite indifferent to the size of their audience. Scarlett saw Alice being tucked into a swing and giggling like a drain as Aristide pushed her and Rome clung to his legs, demanding his turn, and she smiled, aware that he was struggling to work out how to handle both children at once without disappointing either. She was seeing a side of Aristide she had never thought to see, a more laid-back, open side as he grinned at Rome screaming his way down the slide and then stamping with delight through a muddy puddle.

It really wasn't that long before the twins' boundless energy drained away and Rome cried when his increasing clumsiness led to him falling off the short slide steps. Alice sobbed when Scarlett lifted her out of the swing to give another child an opportunity.

'So, this is when they need a nap,' Aristide gathered, scooping up a complaining Rome in one powerful arm and heading back towards the car.

In truth, Aristide was shell-shocked by the experience of meeting his son and daughter properly for the first time. They were much livelier and more demanding than he had innocently expected, and he was unnerved whenever they fell over even when they were playing on a safe surface. His heart lurched inside him when Alice viewed him through tear-drenched green eyes full of distress. Rome simply sobbed and clutched at him, but two minutes later was willing to forget his annoyance at having fallen when something bright and shiny inside the car attracted his attention. It was Aristide's phone and he handed it over like a lamb to the slaughter until Scarlett filched it from him, substituted her own and located a toddler game for her son's use.

'Isn't he a little young for that yet?' Aristide remarked uncertainly.

'Yes, it's a fix for fraught moments only,' Scarlett told him.

Aristide was only now grasping just how much he had missed of their development. Rome and Alice were already little people with distinct personalities and as different from each other as he and Daniele had once been. He worked hard at suppressing his bitterness and his biting sense of injustice, knowing that such feelings would only cause damage in their current situation and that the clock could not be turned back. He accepted that he was still a stranger to his own children, that they hadn't even known what to call him and Scarlett had introduced him by his first name.

'I'm your *papà*,' he had told Rome in immediate contradiction at the playground, and he had seen the pink scoring Scarlett's cheeks at what she took as a rebuke even though it had not been intended as one.

'No more pretending,' he had said to Scarlett then, bright green eyes level and direct. 'There's been too much of that already and I don't want to confuse them.'

Scarlett knew he had had the right to say that to her, but a part of her tender heart burned with regret for the virtual burial of Luke's short-lived role as a father. Intellectually, she knew and accepted that Rome and Alice barely remembered Luke now and that she had to move on and adapt to a changed parental role as well.

Alice clutched Aristide's arm as though she were afraid he would disappear while Rome made another stab at getting Aristide's phone, only grudgingly accepting his father's occasional intervention. For the first time ever, she was not the centre of her children's attention and it stung a little.

While the twins were down for a nap in their cots, she made coffee for Aristide.

'So,' she said chattily and with more cheer than she actually felt as she sat down opposite him. 'How do you see you and the twins developing a relationship?'

'Something normal,' Aristide said rather drily. 'And the way everything's arranged now and the children are living, it's not normal.'

Her mouth ran dry. 'I don't see it that way—'

'Of course you don't because this is the system that *you* chose. Grandparents who aren't grandparents in reality and a father who wasn't their father.'

'Edith and Tom really *love* Rome and Alice—'

'I'm not denying that and they appear to be decent people but they will inevitably see less of the children now that I will be part of their lives.'

Scarlett breathed in slow and deep, conscious of Aristide's shrewd scrutiny, determined not to show her dismay at his attitude to her in-laws, whom she was very fond of. 'All I want is what is best for the twins,' she said simply. 'I don't want to be selfish or possessive or to impose my views on you.'

'I'm seeing my legal team tomorrow and we'll do this legally.'

'That's a rather daunting announcement.' Scarlett lifted her chin. 'For the moment, can't you just get to know the children without all the legal stuff complicating things?'

'I need Rome and Alice to have my name.'

'I understand that,' she conceded. 'But I'm completely willing to be flexible about access arrangements for you to get to know the children.'

Aristide released his breath in a sudden hiss of frustration and leant back, lean strong face taut, jawline stiff, green eyes sharp as blades. 'It will be rather difficult for me to accomplish that. You live on the wrong side of the city. I travel a lot and, while I will naturally try to spend more time in London, it is not my home even if my business headquarters is based here. How am I supposed to become a father on a daily basis, rather than a visitor who simply arrives with gifts and offers occasional adventures?'

'I'm not sure that there's any way that you *can* accomplish that now,' Scarlett admitted with a harried look of regret. 'But I don't see how bringing in the legal profession will change that at present because the twins are too young to do without me.'

'I'm not trying to separate you from them,' Aristide censured quietly. 'I'm not stupid. I can see how much you are their safe place and that my relationship with them will only be enhanced by your presence.'

Scarlett swallowed hard and nodded, not quite sure where the dialogue was heading but a little less unnerved after that concession on his part.

'That's why I want to ask you and the twins to move into the townhouse with me. The school term has ended and you're free for the summer. If you're all living with me, I can build a more normal family relationship with them before you return to work.'

The breath rattled in Scarlett's throat because, once again, Aristide had blindsided her with a proposition she had been wholly unprepared to receive.

'When I'm working I rely a lot on Edith and Tom for childcare and that only works well because I live here. I'm afraid that living with you would be too difficult for me, especially after what happened between us in Italy,' she dared to remind him through lips that felt stiff.

'I'm not changing my mind about what I said earlier. We can't be together as a couple, but I believe we both have enough sense and concern about the children's welfare to act like adults for their benefit,' Aristide intoned.

Her mouth ran dry, a flare of pure panic rippling up through her tense body. 'No, I'm not doing it. I need my own space. I'm entitled to my own space. I'm not moving into your townhouse for you. That would be very uncomfortable for me. You're my ex!' she reminded him thinly, her voice rising in spite of her attempt to control her volume. 'The answer is *no*, Aristide. I'm not giving up anything more because you've given me a guilty conscience over the choices I made two years ago!'

Anger lent a reckless glitter to Aristide's lean, hard face. 'Then we go the legal route and we do everything by the book.'

'You make that sound like a threat,' she condemned unevenly. 'I've bent over backwards to try and make amends, but I can't let you take over my entire life!'

'Is there a boyfriend in the background?' Aristide enquired flatly.

Furious with him now, Scarlett sprang upright. 'No, of course there isn't and you should know better than to ask that question after I was with you in Italy! Whatever else I am, I'm not a cheat—'

'Yet you were quite happy to let *me* think you *were* for two years,' Aristide reminded her in a harsh undertone. 'You didn't care what I thought of you then, when you told me you were marrying Luke!'

Disconcerted by that unwelcome reminder, Scarlett made an awkward movement with one hand. 'That was different—'

'I don't see it as different. Why do you think I'm challenged to trust you in any field now?' he asked curtly, his attention locked to her full pink mouth as the tip of her tongue ran across her lower lip to moisten it. He shifted position, hunger stabbing through him like a secret silent menace.

'I agreed to be your partner at the party. I even agreed to the fake engagement but when is enough *enough* for you? It stops here and now,' Scarlett spelt out in furious warning, evidently impervious to the same susceptibility afflicting him, a reflection that could only incense Aristide more. 'I won't let you intimidate me into doing what I don't want to do!'

'I'm not trying to intimidate you. I'm trying to be reasonable,' Aristide flashed back at her. 'You created this horrible situation for us all and now I'm attempting to fix it the best way I can without injuring or intimidating *anybody*.'

Scarlett nodded slowly, sapphire-blue eyes suddenly wounded and accusing, dark colour warming her pallor. 'It takes two to create a situation, Aristide, and two years ago, you played a part in that situation that you are very reluctant to acknowledge. Whose fault was it that I was *terrified* of telling you I was pregnant even though it wasn't my fault? You see in black and white with no shades of grey. You spent our entire relationship warning me that I was only a temporary aberration in your life. I lived on my nerves with you and you *made* our relationship work that way.'

Aristide had paled and tensed in receipt of that candid comeback. 'I was determined to be honest with you at the time. When I said I didn't want to get married or have children until I was much older and more mature, it was the truth. It never crossed my mind that you could conceive because we were both responsible. Don't hold me to account for not foreseeing that development and the risk that you might choose to take *all* choice away from me.'

'It doesn't matter now.' Scarlett backtracked at speed, afraid that she had exposed herself too much and determined not to get any deeper into a pointless argument that would benefit neither of them.

As Scarlett sank back into her seat, she felt utterly defeated by the abyss of understanding that separated them until she collided without warning with a sizzling green glance from Aristide. A look so hot it should have burned her alive from the inside out. It shook her, that sneaky, momentary glimpse of what Aristide was trying so badly to hide from her. The same male who had rejected her that very morning still *burned* with hunger for her.

It was a revelation, a reassurance that Aristide was not anything like as cold and in control as he liked to pretend he was. He hadn't spent the night making mad, passionate love to her out of revenge or to release his stupid tension, he had spent the night making mad, passionate love to her because he *couldn't* keep his hands off her. Scarlett revelled in that little insight, that decided shift in the power base between them, angling back her shoulders a little, madly aware of the almost compulsive cling of his smouldering gaze to her every movement.

A smile slowly stole the stiffness from Scarlett's luscious mouth. Aristide stared with wary glittering green eyes, taken aback by that switch of mood but also utterly gripped by it.

'I'll *think* about moving into the townhouse,' she told him with quiet emphasis, startling herself almost as much as she startled him with that change of heart but in the space of a moment, in the space of seeing that look of need, of hunger in his gaze, everything had changed for Scarlett. 'But in return, you'll have to rethink your dismissive attitude to Edith and Tom. They're my family now. Our ties go deep. They became a second home for me from the moment Luke and I became friends in primary school.'

'I wasn't aware the ties went that far back.'

Scarlett wrinkled her little nose and smiled again. 'You were never much interested in the finer details of my life.'

Aristide almost winced at that revealing crack but her forgiving smile eased the sting. He recognised the truth of the criticism. To keep part of himself detached, he avoided the kind of emotional intimacy that others took for granted. He didn't let anyone close since Daniele's death, but he had let Scarlett come much closer than most. And look where *that* had taken him, he acknowledged with barely suppressed bitterness.

'I love Edith and Tom and the twins love them,' she continued quietly. 'They're the twins' grandparents and I want them to continue to be treated as such.'

'Done...' Aristide agreed straight away, struggling to understand what had changed inside her, what was making her smile back at him.

Sometimes Scarlett gave him whiplash, but he didn't much care at that moment because she had stopped fighting with him and resurrecting the past he couldn't stand to even think about, never mind relive. Furthermore, she had promised to 'think' about moving into the townhouse. And he wanted that, *her* and his children in *his* house, he wanted it so freaking badly that it was literally *all* that he could think about. He didn't understand it but he was past caring about understanding the urges and thoughts that attacked him in Scarlett's radius.

What was most important now, he told himself soothingly, was gaining the best chance possible to get to know Rome and Alice. Nothing else could or should matter at this stage, never mind whatever hoops Scarlett planned to put him through. There would definitely be hoops ahead, he reckoned, because he recognised that tricky glimmer of challenge in her lovely eyes and wondered where she was planning to take him with it.

'Move in with him?' Brie echoed in horror some hours later as the two young women shared a bottle of wine in Scarlett's living room. 'Which one of you is out of his or her mind?'

Scarlett laughed, convinced she had already experienced the worst that Aristide could do to her after that dismissal in Italy. She refused to believe that he had any plan to take their children away from her. He wanted to share Rome and Alice. He wanted to learn how to be a father. He wanted to forge his own relationship with them. She saw those objectives as perfectly normal and understandable.

'Moving in with separate bedrooms,' Scarlett extended in wry explanation. 'Not quite as groundbreaking a move as it may have sounded.'

'Well, I think it is,' her friend admitted, still shaking her head in astonishment. 'One minute you're doing the fake party girlfriend thing, the next he's stuck a ring on your finger and a split second after that, he's attempting to move you into his home—'

'I only said I'd *think* about it,' Scarlett reminded her friend. 'I haven't fully decided yet. Aristide likes and expects things to happen at the speed of light. I intend to make him wait.'

'You're getting your own back,' Brie assumed with a chuckle.

'Not in any way that could make anything more difficult between us,' Scarlett qualified, although she knew that she wasn't quite telling the truth because she had already made up her mind.

The school term was finished. They would move in. Aristide would get to play *papà*. Scarlett would get to work out what made Aristide tick, what was causing the stop-start sequence he had begun, because there was absolutely something wrong when a male famed for his cool decisiveness blurred the lines over and over again.

Maybe it was simply that he couldn't forgive her for marrying Luke and keeping his children a secret. Only she didn't think that there was anything exactly simple about the way Aristide thought and reacted. After all, there never had been. He had often said one thing to her and then done another, which hadn't given her very clear signals to follow in their previous relationship. He was a mystery and she was done with him being a mystery.

Mid-morning the following day she phoned him at the office. 'Er… Aristide?'

'Did it arrive yet?' he demanded with all the eagerness of a schoolboy.

Scarlett swallowed hard because she really didn't want to disappoint him. Edith was still in stitches in the kitchen over the size of the jungle gym/playhouse that Aristide had evidently purchased for the twins to play on.

'It's arrived,' Scarlett confirmed, grimacing as she glanced at the busy suburban street outside where the massive structure on a low loader and a crane were still snarling up the traffic. 'But I'm afraid there's a problem. It won't fit. It's far too big for the back garden. Put it in your garden at the townhouse.'

'I can't. I bought two of them,' Aristide responded in a clipped undertone.

'Then donate it somewhere where children don't have that kind of outside equipment,' she advised. 'It was a very generous gesture, Aristide, but you over-estimated the size of the garden.'

'My apologies,' he breathed tautly. 'I'll be in touch.'

Scarlett winced as the phone call ended, having sensed his regret and feeling that rare failure for him. She was too soft, way too soft, she warned herself irritably. Before she could think better of the impulse she picked up her phone and texted him a concise list of the sort of toys and equipment that the children were currently able to use.

I can work with this. Thanks.

Relief spread through her and an hour later a beautiful bouquet of flowers arrived for her. Her eyes prickled at the familiar AA signature. She breathed in deep and slow. No, she wasn't about to get sentimental about this, wasn't going to risk catching feelings again. She had been so miserable for so long without Aristide...

But she had had to hide it and internalise her pain because Luke had believed that a wedding ring and a willing father to her twins were the perfect, complete cure for all that emotional stuff, only regrettably they hadn't been. Luke had never been in love, and he hadn't understood what losing the love of her life had felt like. And she wasn't returning to that better forgotten phase of her life when just getting up in the morning with a determined smile had proved a massive undertaking.

She had adapted to life *without* Aristide Angelico and this time around, once she got the new structure for their co-parenting efforts smoothly organised without some cut-throat legal eagle taking charge, she would return to normal. Well, a sort of *new* normal, she adjusted, now that Aristide would inevitably be part of the arrangement and on the outskirts of her life in the future.

More flowers arrived from Aristide the next morning and then an invitation to an exclusive restaurant for dinner the following evening. How could a guy be so sophisticated, successful and intelligent and yet remain so emotionally detached that he did not recognise that that kind of invite was inappropriate in their circumstances? They weren't dating any more. Neither flowers nor invites of that sort were suitable. It was like dealing with a split personality because Aristide *said* one thing and *did* another.

Swallowing hard, she turned down the dinner proposition even though with every fibre of her being she was longing to see Aristide again. Feed a cold, starve a fever, she recited the lesson to herself. Aristide came closest to being a fever in her bloodstream and she refused to put herself out there to be devastated again.

A week later, and only the day before she and the twins were organised to move into Aristide's home, Scarlett returned from some last-minute shopping to be greeted on her own doorstep by Edith.

'You have visitors,' she whispered in a hiss. 'Aristide's mother and some man.'

Scarlett went cold at the thought of Elisabetta Angelico in the sanctuary of her home and she knew that it could mean nothing good. Aristide had made no mention of the older woman having plans to visit and he had already visited three evenings to see Rome and Alice. Of course, Scarlett had endeavoured to stay out of his way during those visits, reluctant to let those boundaries get blurred again.

'Shall I take the twins upstairs?' Edith murmured. 'Or do you want to introduce them?'

Scarlett actually shuddered at that suggestion. 'Upstairs,' she said through numb lips, feeling that her children would be safer unseen by Aristide's unpleasant parent.

Foolishly conscious of her jeans and plain top, her unstyled hair and *au naturel* face, Scarlett squared her shoulders as Edith wheeled the twins in their buggy to the side of the house and her own entrance.

An untouched tea tray with biscuits sat on the coffee table. Edith had tried to be hospitable, and it had been rejected, Scarlett surmised. Elisabetta stood by the window, a rigid figure in a purple designer dress and jacket teamed with enough diamonds to sink the *Titanic*. Aristide's mother was very wealthy, and she liked people to know it. Beside her stood an older man with an air of solemnity much like an undertaker, dressed in an immaculate suit. A professional of some kind, she assumed. A bodyguard?

'Finally,' Elisabetta stressed with impatience as Scarlett appeared. 'I only waited because that woman said you were on your way home. *Home!'* Tiny beringed and glittering hands lifted in a gesture of derisive dismissal. 'Where you are subjecting my grandchildren to poverty.'

Scarlett breathed in deep. 'Does Aristide know you're here?' she asked quietly.

'You only need to know that *I* will not allow you to *blackmail* my son with his children.' Elisabetta spoke English with a cut-glass accent worthy of a royal and she gave Scarlett a scathing up-and-down glance that made it very clear that she was unimpressed.

'I'm not blackmailing anyone. Aristide and I are engaged,' Scarlett reminded the older woman.

Elisabetta vented a derogatory laugh. 'Did you think I wouldn't guess that that was bogus?' she sniped with satisfaction. 'If you were genuinely reconciled with Aristide, you would be living in his house with his children. I know my son. Nothing less would satisfy him. I also notice that you haven't yet offered to let me even meet my grandchildren. Of course, there's no need: I've already seen them.'

As Scarlett's brow creased in bewilderment, Elisabetta extracted a handful of photos from her little clutch bag and tossed them down triumphantly on the coffee table. Scarlett was appalled to see images of her and the twins in the playground, taken recently and without her knowledge. Angry colour marked her cheekbones.

'What are you doing here?' Scarlett demanded tightly, resolved not to react to the photos when she could do nothing about pictures taken in a public place. Losing her temper with Elisabetta Angelico would be a serious misjudgement.

Elisabetta signalled the older man, who asked if they could all sit down and introduced himself as Mervin Hollanditz of Hollanditz and Associates. Scarlett sank down into a seat, deciding that he sounded like a lawyer and chilled by the suspicion. Unfurling a thick document from a briefcase, he outlined the very generous offer that Mrs Angelico was prepared to make in return for Scarlett signing over custody of her children.

'You can stop right there,' Scarlett advised as the older man momentarily paused for breath. 'Never, ever. That's my answer. No, I don't need to know how much money is on the table. There are some things that money can't buy.'

'You're so oblivious to the world I live in, it's ridiculous,' Elisabetta commented, undaunted. 'Give her proposal two, Mervin.'

Her sidekick threaded through his document and began to outline a shared custody arrangement.

'That's Aristide's business, not yours,' Scarlett objected icily.

'You are so naïve about my son that it's almost adorable,' Elisabetta murmured with caustic bite. 'Aristide is ruthless when he needs to be. Even in Europe there are countries that don't belong to the Hague convention and Aristide owns property everywhere, thanks to his grandfather. That means there is no reciprocal agreement with the UK when it comes to custody cases or…*stolen* children—'

'Mrs Angelico!' the lawyer tried to interrupt in dismay, clearly a law-abiding citizen.

But there was no stopping Elisabetta Angelico in the full flood of her arrogance and her powerful sense of superiority. 'And you can't watch them all the time, can you?' she continued poisonously. 'Accept one of these proposals and you will have nothing to fear.

Walk away from both and, trust me, you will learn to *live* in fear and regret.'

As her visitors departed, Scarlett's tummy had succumbed to a queasy roll and she was pale because she knew how very rich Elisabetta Angelico was and how formidable an adversary that made her. She knew that unscrupulous people could be paid to do immoral things like stealing innocent children. She knew that she didn't live in a perfect world. She knew that there was a genuine danger, just as she knew that while Aristide hadn't qualified for a cosy dinner, he was about to receive a visit at his office in the middle of his working day...

CHAPTER EIGHT

ARISTIDE STUDIED THE text and frowned.

Your mother visited me with a lawyer. I'm coming to your office to tell you what it was about.

Aristide was startled and he did something he rarely did. He called his father, Riccardo, to see if he could shed some clarity on the mystery because Aristide could not think of a single *good* reason why his mother might have visited Scarlett. It was not as though she particularly liked children of any age, having only agreed to entertain her own single pregnancy in the first instance because she recognised the need to have an heir to her family fortune.

'One son would have done…but *not* you, you are surplus,' she had once cruelly told Daniele.

At first, Riccardo Angelico had no inspiration to offer, admitting that he had recently seen little of his wife. Only when further pressed had he finally, grudgingly revealed that he was currently in the process of divorcing Elisabetta. 'I wanted to be discreet about it. You know how she is,' he mumbled while Aristide sat back in his chair in shock at that revelation that the worm had finally turned but was predictably staying well out of reach of the bomb he had thrown without warning into the family circle.

Aristide was well aware that a divorce would send his snobbish mother into a violent tailspin of outrage, disbelief and mortification. Nobody cared more about social appearances than Elisabetta Angelico. Nobody had ever been more scathing about other couples who divorced. At best she might have agreed to a separation, but never a divorce. Yet she deserved the divorce, he acknowledged grimly. His father wasn't a bad man, merely a weak man, but bad things had happened to his children on his watch and Aristide found it a challenge to forgive him for it.

Even so, Elisabetta had got thirty-odd years out of her compliant husband and even Aristide felt that Riccardo had paid his dues for marrying for wealth when his own father had demanded that he do so. After all, it was not as though the marriage had ever been a normal one. It was hard to respect a man, however, who bent over backwards to placate bullies and live an easier, more affluent life. Yet he had forgiven his twin for that same weakness, conscience reminded him. Aristide was never keen to concede that, while he might physically bear a close resemblance to his father, he had inherited his essential strength of character and hard, calculating streak from the mother he despised.

* * *

Scarlett had been tempted to rush straight out of the door and erupt into Aristide's office like a woman who had narrowly escaped a catastrophe, but she had more pride and control than that. She changed into the lavender shift dress she had worn the day he gave her the engagement ring and dabbed on a little make-up. She didn't need to embarrass him by appearing in public looking like a wreck, even if wrecked was how she felt in the wake of Elisabetta's insinuations and threats. But nothing could convince Scarlett that Aristide was equally involved in that display of menace. Did she still have too much faith in him?

The new Angelico office building in London was an impressive gleaming tower of glass and she was greeted in the marble foyer by a security man and escorted up to the top floor in what appeared to be a private lift. From the moment she stepped out of it again she was conscious of the attention she was receiving and belatedly she was even more relieved that she hadn't simply rushed out in her jeans. She was supposed to be Aristide's future wife. She only wished that his mother had believed in that fiction because, had she done so, it would surely have kept her at bay.

Aristide was pacing along the floor-deep windows filling his office with light. Tall, dark and stupidly, ridiculously handsome. She didn't think it was a character failing when, even in the midst of her heightened emotions, she felt a suppressed buzz and tightening low in her pelvis and her mouth ran dry. It was merely her unmistakeable constant reaction to him.

'Aristide,' she said a little breathlessly, struggling to regroup and digging into her bag to produce the handful of photos that his mother had left lying on her coffee table and set them down on his immaculately tidy desk.

Aristide frowned down at the photos she had fanned out for his examination and glanced back up at her in bemusement. 'Where did these come from?'

'Your mother had them,' she whispered shakily, quick to plunge right to the heart of the matter. 'She had a lawyer with her as well. She wanted me to sign over custody of the kids or agree to share custody with you—'

Dark fury lit up Aristide's narrowed green gaze like a threatening storm. 'But custody issues are nothing to do with her! She may be their grandmother but that doesn't empower her legally or in any other way.'

'Well, I didn't think so either,' Scarlett continued with greater confidence. 'But she doesn't believe in our engagement—'

'She doesn't need to,' Aristide asserted calmly. 'What she believes is unimportant—'

'I don't think it's quite that simple... I mean, I would like to believe that it is,' she responded in a troubled rush of words. 'But then she mentioned countries that aren't signed up to the Hague Convention, you owning property in such places and *stolen* children.'

Aristide swung away, rage thrumming through him in a lightning bolt of reaction, colour accentuating his slashing cheekbones. It seemed he could fully depend on Elisabetta to destroy any hope he had of gaining access to his children. How dared she imply that *he* would act in such a way?

'I mean, I trusted you. Was that foolish? Would you really consider something like that? Or is this her acting on her own agenda?' she prompted in an anxious surge.

Aristide strode round the desk and reached for both her hands in a sudden powerful movement. 'I swear on my life that I would never ever do something of that nature to you,' he promised in a savage undertone. 'Rome and Alice need your love and attention too much. It's something my brother and I never had and I would be the last man alive to deprive our children of a caring, loving mother.'

That touched her heart because she sensed that response came right from his deepest being, both that admission about Elisabetta and the sentiment he expressed. He was shocked and disgusted by what his mother had done and evidently Scarlett's instinctive trust in his moral values had not been misplaced. The strength of her relief on that score left her feeling almost dizzy. She hung onto his hands for an instant before letting them drop again, needing to recapture her dignity.

'Thank goodness we're moving into your house

tomorrow,' she conceded unevenly. 'I wouldn't feel safe from her threats otherwise.'

'I'm relieved. She's lashing out at you and at me because *her* life is presently being derailed. She's a bully and that's how bullies behave under threat,' Aristide acknowledged in a savage undertone. 'And right now everything Elisabetta most values is being threatened. Her social standing, her role as an arbiter of good taste and refinement, her phoney support for the church. My father is divorcing her.'

Scarlett was thoroughly taken aback by that news but made no comment. She did wonder though if that had anything to do with Riccardo's friendly approach to her at Aristide's birthday party. Had Aristide's father already been embracing the new independence on his divorce horizon and making it clear that he did not share his wife's opinion of her?

Aristide ordered coffee and spoke in Italian on the phone for several minutes. The tension in her stiff shoulders easing a little, Scarlett sat down. 'Are the children safe from your mother?' she pressed worriedly.

'I'm putting security on them,' Aristide admitted as he tossed down his phone.

'But will that keep them safe?' Scarlett continued with a furrowed brow. 'What if one of your security men is bribed or something? Your mother made me very conscious that there are a lot of people out there who could be persuaded to do anything for the right price.'

A tray of coffee was set down on the small table in the corner. Scarlett leant forward from the sofa she was sitting on to pour. Aristide watched her slender dainty hands move back and forth, noting the tremors in them, inwardly cursing his mother for her innate cruelty. He decided to be honest.

'The only guaranteed safeguard I could possibly offer you is marriage. As your husband with shared custody of the children, I could fully protect them,' he confessed. 'Elisabetta is—'

'Crazy as a loon,' Scarlett interrupted apologetically, thinking of how the older woman had slung her warnings with such self-satisfied menace.

'Oh, she's not crazy,' Aristide assured her with a grim darkness shadowing his eyes. 'She's angry, bitter and vicious and, unfortunately, that's her natural state of mind.'

'But why is she like that?' Scarlett whispered with a frown. 'If she was halfway normal, I would have been happy to share the children with her even though she dislikes me—'

'I wouldn't let you. I wouldn't allow her to have access to the twins,' Aristide disconcerted her by admitting. 'She doesn't like kids, couldn't be trusted alone with them. She should never have been a mother. As to why she's like that…after what she did to you today, you deserve the truth.'

Her brow furrowed. 'The…*truth*?'

'When she was a young woman, Elisabetta was actually engaged to my uncle, Stefano, my father's older brother. On a tour of South America, they were attacked and robbed. Stefano was shot dead trying to protect her.'

Scarlett paled, her heart going out to any woman who had endured such a loss. 'She lost the man she loved, I assume—'

'Yes, and it… Riccardo was persuaded into marrying my mother in his brother's stead because both families still wanted the marriage. It was essentially an old-world-new-world connection with the Angelicos providing the class and social status and her family the cold, hard cash,' he told her drily.

'It sounds like their marriage was a disaster in the making right from the start.'

'It was. My parents didn't even like each other and it was never a normal marriage. Daniele and I were test-tube babies made in a lab. I often think that that is why my father could not relate to us. We didn't feel like *his* children. To him we always felt like *her* children and he hated her and didn't take the smallest interest in us.'

'That's very sad,' Scarlett whispered, shaken by the family history he had laid bare and finally understanding why he had never been able to understand the strength of her attachment to her parents or even Luke, who had been the brother she had never had.

'And then there was my twin's experience,' Aristide admitted thickly. 'Daniele fell madly in love with one of his models. It was a very passionate affair but she ran him into debt quite quickly and I urged him to be more careful because I suspected she was only after his money. She moved in with him and then one night at a party he found her having sex with another man. Daniele couldn't handle her infidelity. He had believed that she was perfect and he could neither forgive her nor move on from it. That's why he took his own life.'

'I'm so sorry,' Scarlett murmured softly, full of compassion and hope because it seemed to her that Aristide was finally beginning to trust her when he was willing to confide in her.

Love, family warmth and support hadn't featured anywhere in Aristide's childhood with the single exception of his twin and, tragically, he had lost him as a young adult. He had also grown up witnessing the chilling relationship of his estranged parents and it was hardly surprising that he had decided to stay single until middle age. For a moment she wished she had had access to that background of his years sooner. Only what difference would it have ultimately made? she chided herself ruefully. She hadn't been secure enough with him, hadn't been mature or strong enough back then to step up and tell him about her pregnancy.

'So, where do we go from here?' she asked chattily in the comfortable silence, dipping her chocolate digestive into her coffee and licking off the melted chocolate topping with unselfconscious enjoyment. 'Apart from into your house?'

Aristide shifted in his armchair, murderously aroused by that licking of the biscuit, which took him back years. She had always been the *only* woman to be absolutely herself around him. That quality had been so obvious in her from their first meeting and it had had amazing appeal for a male accustomed to glossy sophisticates.

He watched the tip of that little pink tongue like a hawk and even questioned how he could possibly make the offer he was about to make and stand by it. As his current track record showed, he was no good at resisting Scarlett, in fact he was abysmal at resisting Scarlett. But all the same, he *owed* her because it was his duty to protect her and his children from his lady mother, who was like a shark in the water around those more vulnerable and sensitive.

'I suggest that we go for the marriage option,' Aristide intoned flatly. 'It blocks my mother. She can't touch you as my wife and she won't dare to try and snatch the kids—'

'But why would Elisabetta act against *you*? I thought she adored you.'

'Only when I do what she wants, and I don't any more. I started this bout in the war between us, Scarlett. When I showed up at the party with you on my arm, it was the same as waving a red rag at a bull. I set her off and I did it deliberately,' he admitted in a tone of frustration and regret. 'Because I don't like her and I annoy her whenever I can. If I can strike back in even a small way, it helps me live with what she did to my brother.'

This was Aristide unveiled, admitting stuff he would once never have thought of sharing with her, and Scarlett was transfixed by every word he spoke. 'I can understand that.'

'Can you? Daniele loved her and never stopped looking for love from her even though she despised him. He didn't understand my attitude.'

'But I do. Maybe he saw an idealised version of her as she might have been if life hadn't tripped her up when she was younger,' Scarlett murmured. 'The marriage option? What did you mean by that?'

Aristide yanked back his wandering thoughts, currently anchored on the shift of her shapely legs as she changed position, roaming upward only to note the faint smudge of chocolate on her luscious lower lip. He tensed, wiping his busy brain clear of all such physical impressions. It didn't ease the pressure pushing against his zip but he needed his concentration back.

'We marry for the sake of the protection it grants you and my children. But that's all. We don't have sex…and then when all of this furore calms down and my *crazy* mother turns her malicious streak onto my father and the divorce she doesn't want, perhaps you and I can better decide where we stand then. But right now, you all need my protection. I must be honest with you. I will not want a divorce. I don't want my children growing up in a divided family.'

Scarlett nodded very slowly but she was drenched by the most ridiculous surge of disappointment, drowning in the sensation. That was the riveting moment when she realised that she was *still* in love with Aristide, even more in love than she had been with him two years earlier. She would've stampeded him to the altar if he had offered her the real thing on the matrimonial front. But he *wasn't* offering her that. He was offering her a lifelong commitment in marriage but still *not* a proper marriage.

'I should say what is it about me that I get two men in a row who want to marry me but don't want to sleep with me!' she riposted lightly, determined not to reveal the pain of yet another rejection from Aristide.

He couldn't forgive her for marrying Luke in the first place, never mind depriving him of the knowledge that she had conceived his children. He wouldn't give her a second chance. He didn't believe in second chances. He didn't do forgiveness either. And how could she blame him? He wasn't in love with *her*. He was only trying to keep them all safe from the kind of madness that Elisabetta Angelico was clearly capable of unleashing on all of them. He knew as well as Scarlett was now learning that, while they remained unmarried, his mother could well try to snatch the children for her own benefit to control her surviving son.

'One of those men was gay,' Aristide pointed out gently. 'I'm not gay but—'

Scarlett lifted a silencing hand in a sudden gesture. 'You don't need to say it a second time. I know it doesn't make sense for us to get involved again. We won't be a real couple.'

'No,' Aristide conceded, strangely unwilling to accept her making that point for him, wondering why that should be so when he should be relieved by her quick understanding.

He wasn't offering her a separation or a divorce in the future. Indeed the mere idea of Scarlett moving on with some other man, who would become a stepparent to his children, turned Aristide's stomach.

'I would suggest a register office civil ceremony for us as soon as it can be arranged.'

Scarlett nodded again, feeling ridiculously like a puppet having her strings pulled, but then there was no room for her to give him an honest response. Yes, she was willing to marry him to keep anyone from threatening her children's safety and security. But no, she didn't want to marry him on false pretences because that would be painful for her to endure. Greater exposure to Aristide was not a good idea for her when her feelings were not returned. Doubtless, however, she would learn to handle it and become accustomed to his proximity.

'There is one point I should make, although I would hope that the independent legal counsel you will have before we marry would also point it out. At present I have no real rights over the twins because I'm not married to you,' Aristide confided, compressing his shapely mouth as he made that frank statement. 'When I am married to you, and once all the DNA testing and putting my name on their birth certificates is done, I will have those rights automatically.'

A wry smile drove the tension from Scarlett's lips. 'You didn't have to tell me that. I already knew it. But I always expected to agree to sharing custody with you. It wouldn't be fair to do anything else now that you know you're their father.'

Aristide veiled the surprise in his eyes by bending to reclaim his coffee. He had believed that that fact could be a sticking point for her, which was why he had brought it up in advance. Her easy acceptance shook him because he inhabited a world where nobody ever gave up an advantage without demanding something in return. It also revealed that Scarlett had a greater generosity of spirit than he had shown her over past events.

Faint discomfited colour scored his hard cheekbones. He asked himself where that generosity had gone two years earlier when she had condemned him out of hand and walked away. And there was no satisfying answer to that conundrum. Maybe some time, he reflected hesitantly, he should talk to her about that. As quickly as he considered that idea, he discarded it again.

Some men might share their worst experiences. Aristide wasn't one of them and he remained proud of the fact. There was no point parading old wounds when it was too late to do anything about them. He was pragmatic about such matters. How could he be anything else with a mother like Elisabetta, who had ensured that his and his brother's childhoods had been a nightmare? Daniele had been a nervous wreck by the age of eleven but Elisabetta's spiteful tongue and behaviour had simply hardened Aristide, filling him with a fierce desire to find his freedom and keep it for as long as he possibly could.

Scarlett was studying her fake engagement ring, reckoning there would soon be a fake wedding ring beside it, giving her a perfect phoney pair. She should *not* be thinking overly romantic thoughts, such as what an amazing coincidence it was that Aristide should have given her an engagement ring she adored, if it wasn't real, well, real in the sense of being an expression of love and caring. It was the round setting that she preferred, not too large for her relatively short fingers and it was a sapphire surrounded by diamonds, which she loved as well. No doubt the wedding ring would be equally perfect, a simple display of Aristide's essential good taste, she thought limply.

'I'll have the wedding organised asap,' Aristide told

her briskly, shooting her out of her far too sentimental reflections with a vengeance.

He sounded unemotional, practical, both traits that Aristide excelled at exhibiting.

Once he had ignored St Valentine's Day, seriously disappointing her at the time because it had been the first such holiday when she had had an actual boyfriend. He had also never given her flowers until recently. Instead, he had given her loads of sexy lingerie and jewellery that she suspected was so expensive it would give her a heart attack to know the cost of it. Those kinds of gifts had made her feel rather like the secret mistress of a rich married man, underlining her insecurity about a relationship that appeared to be travelling exactly nowhere.

'It's an unconventional choice but it suits you amazingly well,' Brie chorused admiringly as Scarlett twirled in her electric-blue wedding dress twelve days later. 'And this house is totally amazing. I'm envying the socks right off you right now!'

Scarlett aimed a still appreciative glance at her opulent, highly comfortable surroundings. Even a guest room was three times the size of her former bedroom. It was over ten days since she had moved into Aristide's townhouse with the twins to discover that Aristide had already hired Estelle, a nanny from a famous college, to help out.

She had had an argument with him on the phone

about that piece of bossy interference. Aristide had got her to agree to his requests, had accompanied her to the legal meetings required for their matrimonial plans and had then taken off to New York on business for what remained of the week. By the time he had finished describing the nanny's excellent security training should any kind of threat arise, however, she had had to agree with the friendly young woman's employment. Mercifully, though, there had been neither sight nor sound of Aristide's mother since Scarlett and the children had moved out of the apartment.

'I still think that you could've gone for the white or the parchment shade,' Edith told her regretfully. 'I mean, when you and Luke got married in church, you wore a plain short dress—'

'Only because I looked so pregnant,' Scarlett reminded her. 'And my parents were so embarrassed about that, I didn't want to add to their stress by sporting a wedding gown because they wouldn't have approved of that either.'

'They were so out of touch with young people today,' the slender blonde sighed in recollection and then she glanced up and winced. 'My word, I'm sorry, Scarlett!'

'No need to apologise when it's the truth!' Scarlett laughed.

'I'm just disappointed on your behalf that you never got to do the whole bridezilla thing,' Edith lamented.

Scarlett laughed again, thinking that Aristide would be taken aback quite sufficiently by the sight of her in her long lace and beaded gown and all her diamond and sapphire jewellery. Brie excused herself to change her shoes in the room next door.

'And he may even be a little disappointed too,' Edith murmured. 'I mean, the man's besotted with you. I saw that at first glance.'

Scarlett raised her brows in silent disagreement as she bent her head to slide her feet into her high heels. She hadn't told her in-laws the truth about their marriage, deciding that they would be happier to remain in ignorance of Elisabetta's threats and to believe that she was moving in with Aristide and marrying him for all the normal reasons.

'It made me feel guilty,' Edith admitted. 'If he *always* felt that way about you, we were wrong encouraging Luke to marry you—'

'Oh, stop worrying,' Scarlett urged the older woman with warm affection in her eyes. 'Aristide was *not* in love with me two years ago. I may not know much but I do know that.'

'I hope you're right, because if it *was* the other way—'

'Of course, it wasn't. Marrying Luke was not a mistake,' Scarlett declared confidently to ease her companion's anxiety. 'Luke was there for me when nobody else was and I'll never forget that.'

Arriving at the register office for the ceremony, it was a challenge for Scarlett to look at anyone but Aristide. It might have been a civil ceremony but Aristide had invited his friends, Christine and Matteo Moretti, just as Scarlett had brought along Edith, Tom and Brie. Greetings exchanged, she went back to feasting her attention on the bridegroom, dangerously elegant and sexy in a sleek silver-grey suit of unmistakeable Italian cut. Encountering glittering green eyes, she smiled.

Aristide decided on the spot that Scarlett looked amazing in that colour and wearing all the jewellery he had once bought her. Copper hair tumbled round her shoulders framing her vivacious face, blue eyes as bright as the sapphires she wore with such panache. His broad chest tightened and he had to snatch in a deeper breath.

And then the atmosphere changed as the doors were swung wide to allow the entry of another small, rigid figure. Involuntarily, Aristide froze and then he strode forward to deal with the problem.

'I'll never forgive you if you marry her,' Elisabetta warned him tremulously. 'She's nobody, she's nothing—'

'You're only welcome here if you're prepared to congratulate us after the ceremony,' Aristide murmured quietly. 'I don't want any drama spoiling my wedding day and if you attempt to intervene you will be carried from the premises, which would be embarrassing with the paparazzi waiting outside.'

High colour bloomed over Elisabetta's thin cheeks. 'I will no longer recognise you as my son,' she threatened.

'I'll live,' Aristide riposted as he strode away again.

CHAPTER NINE

SCARLETT WAS THINKING drowsily of that scene before the ceremony as she curled into her comfy bed on-board Aristide's private jet.

Aristide had insisted that they had to enjoy, at the least, a long weekend away after the wedding to look 'realistic'. Edith and Tom were taking care of the twins with Estelle and staying at the townhouse. Scarlett had not understood why Rome and Alice couldn't come with them as well but, on a flight that was to take something in the region of fourteen hours, she could see little point in exhausting their children with such a journey. Where on earth were they heading? Apparently, Aristide was keen to surprise her and she wasn't good enough at geography or flight lengths to make a good guess. But she did naturally think that it was far too long a trip to make for the sake of only three days. She hadn't said so though, indeed had studied to be diplomatic for once in her life.

Why?

Aristide had given her a lovely wedding day, even if it was a fake one. He had got rid of his ghastly mother without an ounce of hesitation. He had given her a platinum plaited wedding ring that was beautiful, informed her that she looked 'utterly gorgeous' in her dress and then kissed her chastely on the cheek after they were pronounced man and wife… Well, nothing was perfect. Afterwards, they had all returned to the townhouse to eat a wonderful meal and Aristide had treated Edith and Tom Walker exactly as though they were her parents—with respect and warmth and acceptance. And for that alone, she was hugely grateful to him.

There was something vaguely familiar about the small airport they landed at and her forehead furrowed as she tried to make the connection. Still slightly somnolent, after the past tiring days, she smoothed down her sundress and climbed into the SUV beside Aristide.

'You're going to love this surprise,' he assured her confidently.

They were married now, she registered, with that faint sense of wonder that only a very new wife experienced. If only it had been a *real* marriage, her comforter of a brain added, and she hushed it immediately. Her children were safe now from Aristide's mother's machinations. Nobody was likely to steal them, least of all Aristide. That was sufficient good news, she assured herself, determined to embrace a bright outlook and enjoy a couple of days in the sun while maintaining good-natured relations with the husband who wasn't really a husband. She could do platonic, of course, she could.

She still hadn't worked out where they were, Aristide noted, feeling very satisfied by that because it would make the surprise even bigger. He was doing everything he could to express his gratitude at the trust she had shown him in agreeing to marry him. A new holiday wardrobe awaited her at the villa, a wedding gift of jewellery on her bed, flowers everywhere because she loved flowers, and his housekeeper would have breakfast waiting for them on the terrace.

Scarlett smiled to herself. He couldn't have brought her back to the island of Dominica where they had spent their very first night together. That had been an outrageously romantic experience from start to finish even if Aristide couldn't have intended it that way. No, even Aristide had to be too intelligent to walk her back through those particular recollections when everything between them was now so different, Scarlett reasoned frantically.

He angled the vehicle down a steep lane, clearly newly planted up with tropical vegetation, and then she saw the even more familiar green roof, although that looked very much more extensive than she recalled, but still her heart was beginning to beat very, very fast in consternation.

'We're on Dominica,' Aristide announced with all the pizzazz of a showman pulling an entire flock of white rabbits out of a magician's hat.

'At the same villa…is it?' she queried in shock.

'Yes, you loved it here…loved the island as well,' he reminded her with vast insensitivity.

'Oh, this is a wonderful surprise!' Scarlett gasped with fake enthusiasm when, truly, she just wanted to slap him and scream at him to get with the new platonic programme.

'I've made some improvements since my grandfather's passing and I extended the house,' Aristide informed her chattily as he escorted her into the cool tiled, air-conditioned hall. 'This is our housekeeper now—Marthe. Her mother, Sandrine, has retired.'

A beaming dark-skinned woman presented her with flowers. Scarlett thanked her in schoolgirlish French, a language that Aristide spoke like a native, having spent vacations on Dominica with his grandfather as a boy. Aristide asked her whether she wanted a tour first or breakfast.

'I'm starving,' she confided reluctantly, recognising that she would have to keep her dissatisfaction with him to herself for the sake of peace.

'Me too…'

A guiding hand at her spine, Aristide walked her out to the terrace with its incredible view of the turquoise Caribbean Sea through the gently waving fronds of the palm trees. As she sat down she noticed the twisting torturous track down to the silvery grey strand below had been replaced by steps that looked a good deal safer. But for a split second all she could remember was running down the original path, giggling as Aristide teased her about something, and she had almost fallen and he had caught her to him and kissed her, a deep, endless kiss that had left her tingling and desperate for that something *more* that she had not yet experienced.

'It takes you back, doesn't it?' Aristide guessed, shaking his handsome dark head as if he were remembering as well. 'I know it was only about three years ago but we've both grown up a lot since then.'

'Yes,' Scarlett conceded, because certainly that was true. Aristide seemed a lot more accessible than he had once been and she had no idea how that had come about. And she had matured because she had become a mother and having two babies had irrevocably changed what was most important to her.

She sipped her mango smoothie and selected a stuffed plantain cup filled with tiny segments of fruit, vegetables and meat. Aristide chose a slice of watermelon pizza. She added a Dominican baked roll to her plate and tucked in. 'I put on half a stone the last time we were here.'

Aristide studied her with amused emerald-green eyes that glittered in the sunshine and he just took her breath away in that way he did and nobody else ever had. Lean bronze features, perfectly sculpted and darkly shadowed with stubble round his stubborn, wilful mouth. 'You still looked fabulous. In any case, I've signed us up for a hike this afternoon.'

Oh, joy, she thought ruefully, good, clean, fun for the honeymoon couple since nothing else was on the table. She could look forward to snorkelling and trekking, pastimes guaranteed to exhaust them both and satisfy Aristide's need to be constantly doing something. On her last visit they had spent most of the time on the beach or in bed, fuelling up on snacks to keep up the pace. Back then, though, they had been locked in a powerful bubble of intimacy that now had the power to make her eyes sting with regret: for what they had once had, for what they had lost.

'I'll unpack first, have a shower,' Scarlett told him as she finished eating. 'Would you mind if I didn't do the hike? I sort of just fancy sitting on the beach with a book and being lazy.'

'We can do it tomorrow instead—'

'No, seriously, *you* go. I'm quite happy to be on my own for a few hours,' Scarlett slotted in with resolve.

Frustration currented through Aristide, who did not want to go trekking without her. But hold on, he reminded himself very seriously, this was now, not before when she had once done things she didn't want to do for his benefit. He couldn't expect that any more. Scarlett had been so happy here in the villa almost three years earlier and he had somehow miraculously hoped to recapture that with her.

Was that why he had brought her to the island in the first place? His ebony brows drew together in a frown of perplexity. Now that everything was so different between them, naturally the ambience would also be different. All of a sudden Aristide wanted a very strong drink but even more he wanted to see Scarlett smile again.

'That's fine,' he agreed, and she smiled with the genuine warmth that lit up her whole face like sunshine, and he gazed back at her feeling immensely satisfied by that result even if it did mean doing without her company for several hours.

Which was how things were now, he recalled afresh. He would be damned before he would go back…no, no, he wasn't going there again, he promised himself as scorchingly bad memories threatened to engulf him. With decision, Aristide rose from the table to go and get changed for his three-hour trek to Boiling Lake *without* Scarlett.

Marthe showed Scarlett to her designated bedroom in the new extension. She swept open the door of a built-in dressing room to show off the many clothes already hanging there. For an instant, Scarlett felt a sharp, sick pang in her stomach at the suspicion that Aristide had brought some other woman to Dominica with him and then she noticed the labels still attached and the obviousness newness of the garments and her tummy settled again. Aristide had bought *her* a summer wardrobe.

And that wasn't all he had bought her, she registered in dismay as she was climbing into one of the beautiful bikini sets on offer and finally noticed the substantial gift box waiting for her on the bed, adorned with a card and Aristide's initials. She opened the large, shallow jewellery box and her eyes opened very wide in stunned disbelief. A sapphire and diamond tiara met her gaze. Where on earth did he think she was likely to wear *that* in their pretend marriage? With pursed lips, she anchored it into her hair in spite of the fact that she was wearing a bikini. The tiara looked as stupendous on her as a crown. Well, might as well feel like a queen for the day, she thought ruefully as she gathered up a towel and book to pad down to the beach.

How was she supposed to handle these utterly inappropriate gifts from him? The clothes, yes, she could certainly use them in the short term and could even appreciate that he didn't want his wife garbed in the inexpensive items that comprised her wardrobe. But a tiara? On what planet did Aristide live on that he somehow thought she would have a need for a tiara that had undoubtedly cost him a fortune?

How did she know that? She had once, while she was still with him, had the sapphire earrings he had first bought her valued for the purpose of insurance and she had been shocked and ultimately horrified by how very valuable they were. After that discovery, bearing in mind that she was too poor even to afford the insurance payment, she had been sure to keep all that jewellery at *his* apartment.

Why had he ever spent so much money on those

lavish gifts of jewellery when he wasn't even planning on staying with her? She had never understood that extravagance of his. Yes, she knew he was very wealthy but, even so, there should still have been limits on how much he spent on a casual girlfriend.

Aristide went straight for a shower when he returned from his lone hike. He had wanted to share that experience with Scarlett but sharing anything with him, he was dimly beginning to grasp, was not presently in her repertoire. He recalled how he had behaved in Italy and winced at the inept harshness that only *she* brought out in him. He would have to do better, much better with her, he acknowledged, wishing that life had not suddenly become so very complicated. Why had he promised to behave in a manner which went against his every natural instinct? Could this inner turmoil that he despised while the sheer weight of it tore him apart possibly be *all* his own fault?

That suspicion was enough to push him into pulling on a pair of board shorts and pouring himself a tequila. He strode out onto the terrace to espy Scarlett lying in the shade below the trees edging the beach, her spectacular hour-glass figure displayed in three flimsy colourful triangles. And what was that on her head catching the dappled sunlight as she moved? He grabbed up binoculars and focused them and then he laughed with rich appreciation at the sheer irreverent nonsense of Scarlett sporting her tiara on the beach. Only Scarlett would do that, only Scarlett rejoiced in that kind of individuality. All of a sudden feeling like some kind of a pervert for spying on his bride, he tossed aside the binoculars and had a second drink, because he accepted that he had an awful lot to think about.

Early evening, Scarlett reached the top of the steps that led up from the beach breathless and looked in surprise at Aristide lounging back against the table. 'I thought you were still out,' she confided. 'How was the hike?'

'It was good,' he said non-committally as if it had been miserable, but he was too polite to say so.

'Well, I dozed and read and dozed and read and feel much fresher. We made a long trip for a short stay.'

'Possibly not my cleverest idea,' Aristide breathed, disconcerting her with that admission.

'I'll be out to join you as soon as I have a shower,' Scarlett declared. 'You know, I wasn't criticising. It's beautiful here but—'

'Everything's changed,' Aristide slotted in with measured emphasis, disconcerting her for a second time.

What an odd, introspective mood he was in, Scarlett thought as she peeled off the bikini and walked into the shower to get rid of the sand coating her sticky, sun-lotion-drenched skin. Freshened up, she wrapped a towel round herself and walked back into the bedroom only to find Aristide there examining the tiara she had laid back in its case on the dresser.

'It's exquisite and thank you,' she said awkwardly. 'But it was a weird gift. When would I ever wear it?'

Aristide flipped shut the box and slowly turned round. 'There will certainly be important social occasions for us to attend as a couple in the future,' he intoned. 'It looked amazing on you when you came up the steps, *cara*.'

There was something almost vulnerable darkening his stunning green gaze as he stared at her, his lean, strong face taut, his lean, muscular torso bare above the shorts, and her heart squeezed tight inside her chest. 'What's wrong?' she asked.

'I still want you,' he breathed tautly.

Scarlett almost winced but chose not to lie or pretend. 'I worked that out already.'

Aristide swore under his breath. 'This whole situation I set up is…*wrong*—'

'It's not that bad,' she said soothingly, helpless against her overwhelming desire to comfort him when he was down.

'Being with you, not being able to touch you…*kills* me,' he admitted in a raw undertone, those expressive eyes of his holding her fast as she nibbled uncertainly at her full lower lip.

Her hand rose involuntarily and stretched up towards a strong brown shoulder. 'Me too,' she muttered, wondering as soon as she said it if admitting that was the stupidest idea she had ever had.

His skin was warm and smooth as satin and the scent of him that close was an aphrodisiac. He smelled of sunshine and clean, hot masculinity. Heat curled between her thighs, a hollow ache tugging at the heart of her. Aristide gazed down at her with smouldering desire and a split second later she was tilting her head back, her lips parting in invitation, and thought had nothing to do with either of those actions.

His hard, demanding mouth crashed down on hers with all the passion she craved. Her hands travelled up, tracing his abs, smoothing down his torso to the V-shaped muscles that ran down into his waistband. A shudder ran through his lean, powerful frame and she felt the towel fall away as he backed her down onto the bed to kiss her with mounting, urgent hunger. It was as if she had been starved of him, her arms locking round his neck, her body rising up to his and embracing his weight with a breathless sound of pleasure.

Satisfaction and relief were trilling somewhere in the back of her mind because she knew now that she had read him right when he had asked her to move into the townhouse with him. Aristide wanted her, Aristide had wanted her again from the very beginning of their unconventional reconciliation.

'Staying away from you was crazy,' Aristide growled, shaping her breasts with reverent hands before turning his mouth to her sensitive nipples, making her buck and moan in response under him.

'C-crazy,' she stammered when she caught her breath again.

'And it makes *me* crazy,' he told her, ravishing her pink lips with driving desire, and as their tongues swirled she detected the faint tangy flavour of tequila, which surprised her because Aristide very rarely touched alcohol.

The reflection quickly evaporated from her brain as Aristide bent his head to the apex of her body, dallying there with the electrifying skill of an artist until her heart was pounding, her hips were writhing, and she was pushed into an all-encompassing climax. But that once wasn't enough for him and the dusk light darkened deep until he had wrung several more from her. She surfaced from that boneless surfeit of pleasure slowly, seeing Aristide reach into the nightstand.

'Is this your room?'

'If you weren't here. Your clothes require more space than mine,' he teased, green eyes alight with wicked amusement.

'Well, if you will keep buying me more...'

An ebony brow quirked. 'We'll share now.'

His tone warned her that that was actually a question that she wasn't yet ready to answer. Once again, Aristide had changed everything between them and broken his own rules. He could be the most infuriating male, she thought helplessly, threading fingers happily through his black curls.

'It needs to be cut,' he warned her with a heart-stopping smile. 'So, for that matter, does our son's. He's a little boy.'

'Men wear their hair in all sorts of different styles these days. Long, short, tied back, buns, braids,' Scarlett told him loftily. 'You're just old-fashioned.'

Without warning a frown, his lean, muscular body froze and his lean, darkly handsome features clenched hard. 'This feels like a time slip,' he said curtly. 'We're talking too much.'

And before she could say another word he was kissing her passionately again, rekindling the feverish need that she could not withstand until she was clinging to him, her body lifting inevitably to his. He entered her with the scorching urgency she had never forgotten, filling her in a single slamming thrust. Hunger without conscience rose in her like a leaping flame. Burning heat engulfed her, driving her hips up to receive him. Nothing had ever felt so good, nothing had ever felt so necessary. Tightening bands in her pelvis thrummed with wild excitement and, a little later, the world went white behind her eyelids as the resulting explosion of lusty pleasure took her by storm.

She flopped back on the bed damp with sweat and the lingering pulses of physical bliss. So, they were to share a room now. That was a new beginning, she acknowledged with relief as Aristide slid off the bed with predatory grace and stalked into the bathroom. Then he swung round in the doorway.

'Marthe said dinner would be ready in…' He checked his watch and winced. 'Fifteen minutes left. I'll use the shower next door.'

And with that he was gone and Scarlett flew out of bed and headed to the shower alone, thinking absently of other showers they had shared in the past. Aristide had seemed oddly detached, as if he was locked up inside himself, looking at her without really looking at her.

Or was she being paranoid and looking for problems that weren't there? Why the heck would Aristide be behaving like that when he had gone out of his way to bring intimacy back into their relationship and give them a more normal marriage? Even Aristide could not be on the brink of backing off from her again, could he?

Marthe delivered a banquet of dinner dishes to the big table on the terrace. A net of twinkling fairy lights hung above them.

Aristide strolled out to join Scarlett clad in tailored khaki chinos and a white linen shirt. 'I've made arrangements for you to spend tomorrow at a nature spa being pampered,' he revealed. 'You enjoy that sort of thing.'

Yes, but not in the middle of a very brief honeymoon when it would separate them for another precious day. Was he avoiding her? Or was that a bizarre suspicion?

'Do you know it's only now occurring to me that, although we were together almost a year, we really knew very little about each other,' Scarlett remarked.

Aristide studied his plate. 'We knew pretty much everything we needed to know.'

'I don't agree,' she said in a mild tone. 'It's made such a difference to my understanding of you to know about your background.'

'You sound like a counsellor,' he scoffed lightly, pouring more wine into her waiting glass. 'And I don't do that talking thing. Keeping it all to myself always worked best for me.'

'I think you might understand me better if I told you about my family,' she murmured.

'You said they loved you. What more is there to say?'

'That from when I was tiny I was told what a *lucky* little girl I had been because they had adopted me, and as I got older I was reminded of who knew what horrors I might have endured in an orphanage or with an unsuitable family had they not picked me.'

Aristide sat back and frowned, his lean, strong face taut. 'Nobody should have been saying such things to a child.'

'But people did, and I always felt I owed a duty to my parents to be the young woman they wanted me to be…not the more adventurous and outspoken me that

I actually am,' she framed uncomfortably. 'I worked very hard at being the perfect daughter and it was hard because I didn't think like they did and we'd nothing in common. It wasn't until I met my birth mother—'

'You *met* her?' Aristide incised in surprise. 'When did that happen?'

'When I was eighteen. Crystal had left me a letter on file and I asked her to meet me. It was a bit of a disappointment.' Scarlett grimaced. 'I was kind of looking for an ongoing relationship, but she wasn't. She was perfectly happy with her career and her child-free life but I saw a lot of myself in her. She was stronger than I had ever dared to be, more willing to speak her mind freely. I honestly do think that if I'd been a couple of years older and my parents had been gone when we first met that what went wrong between us wouldn't have gone wrong—'

'I disagree,' Aristide pronounced flatly, his Italian accent very strong.

That was rather a conversational killer, Scarlett conceded, and she gave her full attention to the beautiful meal instead, helping herself to rice balls stuffed with saltfish, crispy chicken wings and mashed breadfruit.

Eventually, Aristide made light conversation and her frustration increased because it seemed that he wasn't willing to discuss anything that might clear the clouds of the past that still hung over them. And those clouds were definitely still hovering, etched in the grim aspect to his taut cheekbones, the troubled light in his eloquent green eyes and his obvious tension. He *couldn't* forgive her, she recognised unhappily. He couldn't forgive her for marrying Luke and staying silent about her pregnancy.

When Aristide finally fell silent, she left him drinking on the terrace, staring broodingly into the darkness.

'Are you coming to bed?' she hung back to ask awkwardly.

His coal-black curls fell back from his perfect profile as he turned to look at her. 'Not yet. I think I'll go for a walk on the beach.'

Scarlett went to bed alone with a troubled heart.

CHAPTER TEN

AT FOUR IN the morning, Scarlett wakened after a bad dream and realised that Aristide still hadn't joined her. Rising, she pulled a beach kaftan over her head and went to check the room next door, but that bed was equally empty, the sheets undisturbed. Having checked the rest of the house for him, she walked out onto the silent terrace still illuminated by the fairy lights and walked carefully down the steps to the beach.

Moonlight lit up Aristide's white linen shirt and the tequila bottle in his hand. Her brow indented. She trudged barefoot through the pale gritty sand towards him. 'What is wrong with you?' Scarlett demanded worriedly. 'It's not like you to drink like this.'

'You might be surprised. Two years ago, I actually followed in my lush of a grandfather's footsteps for an entire two months,' Aristide declared thickly.

'What on earth are you talking about?'

Aristide sprang upright, his sheer height and width almost intimidating as he cast a long dark shadow over her. 'Nothing,' he said flatly.

Scarlett breathed in deep. 'Look, I'm not stupid, Aristide. This is all about the past—what I *did*, what I *didn't* do—and I very much regret it now. I wish you could accept that. I feel guilty...very guilty,' she said shakily, tears clogging her vocal cords. 'But I can't go back and change anything I did. It's too late. All I can say is that I'm truly sorry—'

A humourless laugh escaped Aristide, his eyes glittering dark and colourless in the moonlight. 'You don't understand what you did, though, do you?' he grated soft and low. 'That engagement ring I gave you... I bought it two and a half years ago!'

'Two and a half years ago?' Scarlett repeated, stunned by the reference to that time frame.

'While we were still *together*,' he emphasised, walking along through the surf softly bubbling and swirling onto the sand. 'I know I didn't get around to actually proposing but I'm a very cautious guy with women. I simply waited too long...at least that's what I *used* to think. That you had settled for Walker because he was offering you what you wanted and I had failed to do so. The truth, however, when you gave it to me that day on our flight to Italy and told me about our children, was even *worse*.'

Scarlett fell back from him in shock. He had bought that ring to propose while they were still together? How was that even possible? If that were true, he was telling her something that would blow her whole world and her belief in her own judgement sky-high.

'What are you trying to say? That you had…feelings for me back then?' she pressed dubiously. 'Aristide… turn round and talk to me!'

'I'm drunk.'

'That doesn't matter right now,' she muttered, her fingers closing into the sleeve of the unbuttoned shirt he wore to pull on it.

'It matters to me,' he said flatly. 'My grandfather was a drunk, which is why I rarely drink. My father won't touch a drop.'

'D-did you have feelings for me two years ago?'

'What do you think?' Aristide turned the question back on her. 'We were virtually living together. I didn't slide into that kind of compromising arrangement with a woman without having *feelings* as you call them. However, you're right on one score… I didn't *want* to feel for you what I did feel because, right from the teenage years, I had promised myself that I would never fall in love with anyone.'

'But why?' she whispered almost brokenly.

'My grandfather's two nasty divorces drained the Angelico family fortune.'

'But you said he was an alcoholic and that can't have been easy on his wives,' she pointed out gently. 'You can't only blame the wives for the marriages that failed.'

'Scarlett, always so rational and seemingly so clear-headed.' Aristide saluted her mockingly with his bottle. 'But you didn't even *notice* that I was madly in love with you…'

Scarlett had lost colour and fallen still. 'I still find that very hard to believe because, the whole time we were together, you kept saying stuff like, "*If* we're still together next month…", "I'm *not* going to be with you for ever…", "We're together until one of us gets bored…" and, of course, I always thought that the one who got bored would be you.'

Aristide shifted position. 'So, there were grandfather's divorces, my parents' car crash of a marriage, my own unsavoury experiences with women and finally the nasty piece of work who betrayed Daniele. All of that made me very reluctant to trust a woman and marry and then *you* came along and all my good sense went straight out the window!'

'And that must've been when you bought the engagement ring. But, surprise, surprise…you never *gave* it to me!'

Her heart was breaking inside her. She was convinced that she could hear the roar as every one of her defences crashed because she had loved him so much back then, indeed, had never stopped loving him.

Aristide loosed a bitter laugh. 'I kept putting it off… I was scared. I wasn't sure I was ready. To put it mildly, getting hitched in my twenties wasn't what *I* had ever seen in my future!'

'And then it no longer mattered because I let you down,' Scarlett assumed as the silence dragged while the surf continued to wash their feet. Her face was wet with tears she didn't recall falling from her eyes. 'I was scared too. I ran off and married Luke.'

'That almost destroyed me. I was devastated. Words cannot describe what I went through in the months after that because I trusted you. I thought you cared for me too. It was the worst ordeal of my life... even worse than losing Daniele,' he breathed raggedly.

'And then you drowned your sorrows in a bottle,' she guessed wretchedly. 'That two months you mentioned when I first came down here tonight. Was that then?'

He gazed out over the dark ocean and nodded jerkily.

'I extended the house here for us as well,' he murmured curtly. 'For the future I thought we would have then.'

How do I make this right? she thought painfully. And the chilling answer came back that there was nothing she could do to change the mistakes of the past. But they had both made mistakes, only he didn't seem to see that. He was still too angry, too bitter about the pain she had inflicted when she married Luke. Her heart bled at the concept of Aristide missing her, needing her, wanting her. Oh, what an idiot she had been to run away!

'I ruined everything we had together,' Scarlett conceded heavily, her distress perceptible in the tears sliding down her distraught face. 'Only who knows if you would *ever* have had enough faith in me to actually *give* me that ring? You could have changed your mind. You still didn't trust me enough and even now... Luckily though, knowing what I do now, I understand better. I understand why you said that we could never be a couple and why you backed off from me in Italy again. Only that seems like a loser's game to me, Aristide...and you're not a loser.'

'What are you trying to say?' he demanded starkly, high cheekbones glimmering in the low light, sculpted mouth compressed.

'All that happened a long time ago and we've both changed,' she murmured hoarsely. 'Why can't we have a new start with our children? I still love you. I've always loved you. We could have the world but you're denying both of us that opportunity because you won't give me a second chance and you're bitter...'

The sob trapped in her throat wouldn't let her say any more. She had shot her last bolt, she conceded unhappily. She loved him and evidently he had once loved her, but love wasn't always enough. Their physical attraction remained but possibly that was all there was left on his side now and even she was willing to admit that they would need more to sustain a marriage.

She climbed the steps slowly, carefully, desperate for him to follow her and to take that challenge, that invitation of hers, but she reached the bedroom alone. She closed the door, shed the kaftan and, not even caring about the sand still clinging to her feet, she climbed into bed and cried her heart out for what might have been—if only she had been stronger, more confident, more intuitive and he had been less distrustful and wary.

Thirty minutes later, Aristide glanced quietly into the room where Scarlett slept and withdrew with a sigh after seeing the tear stains on her cheek. Dawn was now sending glowing light and colour into the night sky. He entered the office he had had built and began to make phone calls, work out arrangements and cancel appointments. While he did so, he wondered why it had never occurred to him before that Scarlett was much tougher than he was. Tiny but with a backbone strong as steel and the tenacity of a bulldog.

When Marthe wakened Scarlett for breakfast and explained that she was being picked up soon for her spa trip, she also mentioned that Aristide had only gone to bed an hour earlier and Scarlett forced a smile. Tomorrow they would be flying back home, where they would no doubt be terribly polite to each other for everyone's benefit. She would survive, she told herself fiercely, she had survived losing Aristide once, she would get through it again…eventually. But just then she felt as if Aristide had wrenched her heart out the night before by cruelly telling her of what might have been between them.

The spa day sentenced her to hours of relaxation she didn't want. If she wasn't being coated in mud or some aromatic concoction and being massaged, she was soaking in one of a variety of natural hot-spring pools. Once that was complete she had a manicure and a pedicure and a blow-dry. Only neither the luxury treatments and soaks nor the awareness that she was looking her best improved her mood as she was driven back to the villa while practising her game smile.

Nothing, she decided, could make her feel smaller than having told a man that she loved him and being ignored like a silly child who had said something embarrassing in public. She had buried her pride, launched her thousand ships of persuasion but, sadly, she was no Helen of Troy. Aristide wasn't about to fight for her affections. No, Aristide was far too busy being cool and sophisticated and proud and bitter to see what she saw and that was that they still belonged together.

As she vanished at speed into her bedroom, Marthe informed her that dinner was almost ready. She shed her clothes and walked into the dressing room to select a long fancy dress the colour of a tart green Granny Smith apple. There was no need to bow out of Aristide's arid and unforgiving emotional life like a damp squib. No, she would go with a great big noisy bang. Piece by piece, she donned all the sapphire and diamond jewellery like armour, a not-so-subtle reminder of how much Aristide had once valued her.

Tears stung the backs of her eyes and she blinked them back furiously because she was done crying over the past. He wanted platonic? He wanted a detached marriage? Well, he was about to get platonic and polite with bells on!

Marthe had really pushed the boat out for dinner. The table was set with a cloth and loads of candles and even rejoiced in a picturesque trail of scattered flower petals. Aristide's green gaze locked to her the moment she appeared and he sprang up to pull out her chair.

'You look magnificent,' he told her. 'Let's eat.'

Scarlett rammed down her insecurities when she noticed that he had dressed up as well as though the meal were a special occasion. He wore a tailored dinner jacket and narrow black trousers that enhanced his tall, lean, muscular physique. Only the taut line of his cheekbones and the lines bracketing his passionate mouth warned her that he was very tense.

'Not before time,' Aristide quipped as he poured wine for her and passed her the first serving dish. 'Did you enjoy the spa?'

'Yes.' She began to make selections to fill her plate, her soft mouth down-curving. 'It was a real treat.'

'Since we talked in the middle of the night, I've learned a great deal about my true nature,' Aristide told her very seriously. 'I'm too emotional and very intense, rather like my late twin without, thankfully, his instability. But when I get down in mood, I do tend to wallow in my misery, only last night, you *fixed* me, cured me, whatever you want to call it.'

Her smooth brow indented as she toyed with her delicious food. 'What are you trying to say?'

'That I lost you once and lived to very much regret it…and now I will not allow *anything* to come between us, least of all my own faults.'

'But you're still angry and—'

'I'm not angry any more,' he hastened to declare. 'Last night was a wake-up call for me.'

'Bitter?' she queried with a perplexed frown.

'Not since a certain wonderful woman told me that she still loved me even though I *was* angry and bitter. That very brave woman still loved me even when I was destroying my second chance with her. Still loved me in spite of all the mistakes I made,' Aristide assured her, green eyes bright but anxious resting on her shaken face. 'And it may be hard for you to believe it but, no matter how angry and bitter I was, I still *loved* you as well.'

'Accepting that is a tall order,' Scarlett muttered unevenly.

'The minute I knew you were unattached again, I *had* to see you. Not at the funeral, though, where you would've been grieving for another man, so I made myself stay away until the memorial service. I told myself that I only wanted closure.'

Scarlett studied him with wondering eyes.

'I wouldn't let myself think about what else I

wanted from you, but my real motives still bled through. I came up with my first excuse to get you back into my life when I asked you to come to my birthday party and it just went on from there. By that first morning in Italy, I was determined to get that ring on your finger,' he admitted. 'And finding out about the twins may have made me angry and bitter, but please note that it didn't stop me coming up with all the excuses of the day to persuade you into accepting that ring.'

'You were very smooth about it,' Scarlett commented as she tried to eat, only she was so hyped up, it was a challenge to swallow.

'And then we ended up in bed and I...panicked afterwards. I didn't want you to suspect that I was still in love with you, even though by that stage I was pretty sure that I was being rather obvious.'

'No, you hid it very well,' she conceded. 'And then you asked us to move into your home.'

'I wanted you close and even though I knew it was too soon to ask that of you, I had to try. When my mother came after you, however, it lit a fire under me. I would have done anything to keep you and our children safe from any kind of threat.'

'I realised that, which is why I trusted you enough to marry you.' Aristide reached across the table and laced his fingers with hers and she smiled again, a warm glow rising in her chest because she was beginning to believe, to accept that Aristide could finally be hers.

'But why on earth did you insist on a fake marriage?'

'I was still trying to protect myself from being hurt again. I told myself that I could resist you, but I can't.' Aristide sighed. 'I've never been able to resist you and, by the way, I no longer blame you for running off with Luke.'

'Seriously?' she gasped in astonishment.

'I did purposely keep you on edge throughout our previous relationship,' he acknowledged reluctantly. 'I was too insecure to tell you the truth about my feelings. I didn't want to raise false expectations, so instead I told myself that I was managing your expectations. Ironically it was only the day that you texted me that you were marrying Luke that I realised once and for all that I loved you one hundred per cent—'

Scarlett's eyes stung. 'I must've hurt you so much. I didn't realise that I *could* be that important to you then. I had accepted that I was just a casual girlfriend who would never be anything more. I didn't want to land you with the responsibility for a pregnancy I believed you wouldn't want...and Luke *did* want my babies.'

'I made the biggest mistake of my life when I didn't confront you about that text. I was too proud. Instead I chose to believe that you must've had something going on with Luke while you were still with me. It was pride and anger and jealousy and nothing more important that kept me away from you. When you finally told me about the twins, I was shocked out of my skull.'

'I know, but you did try *really* hard to deal with it,' she said softly.

'I did and I didn't. I got hung up on what I had lost out on rather than what I had *gained*,' Aristide reasoned with regret. 'In one sense it was a slap in the face finding out about our children because we could have had our happy ending without Luke, if even *one* of us had had the courage to tell the other the truth two years ago.'

'I never thought of that angle but it's true. If I'd admitted that I was pregnant then, you might have told me that you loved me after you got over the shock of learning that you were an expectant father,' Scarlett conceded ruefully.

'So, now I do what I should have had the guts to do two years ago,' Aristide pronounced, clasping her hand to raise her upright.

In bewilderment, Scarlett watched him get down on one knee in front of her. 'What are you doing?'

'Will you marry me…*again*? In a proper church, wearing a ravishing white dress, because I want you to have that experience. I've deprived you of enough. I want to start this reconciliation on a high, positive note.'

'But we can't get married twice over—'

'No, but we can have a blessing and all our friends

present to see us get married the way I should have married you the first time.'

Scarlett tapped a toe with a huge smile, happiness dancing through her like shards of sunlight. 'Do I get a real honeymoon next time?'

Aristide groaned. 'Well, we're getting the honeymoon *ahead* of the church blessing,' he explained. 'I phoned Edith and Tom this morning first thing and asked them and the twins and the nanny to fly out here and join us tomorrow. Tom spoke to his partner and has freed himself up for two weeks, so all the arrangements have been made. I've rearranged my schedule and you're already free. We're very fortunate that I extended this house.'

Scarlett flung her arms round him in wonder and excitement. 'Edith, Tom and Rome and Alice will be with us tomorrow? Oh, that's wonderful news…it'll be like a family holiday!'

'Which means that if I want to chase you naked round the house, it *has* to be tonight while we're still alone,' he warned her teasingly.

'I'll meet you down on the beach,' she promised as she laced her hands round his neck to pull his head down to hers. 'And you're still going to keep on getting your curls shorn, aren't you?'

'Yes…won't lie about that,' he declared with amusement.

'Give me five minutes,' she urged, but he locked her to him and kissed her with hungry fervour.

'You'll need my help to get all that jewellery off.'

Scarlett just laughed. 'You'd grab any excuse to follow me into the bedroom right now.'

'A man should only marry a woman who knows his weaknesses.'

Scarlett grasped the hand that had reached out to enclose hers in a possessive hold. 'That is not a weakness. It tempted you out of suppressing your feelings and made it possible for you to share how you truly felt tonight. I was brave last night. Tonight it was your turn.'

'I almost wakened you this morning to admit that you had brought me to my senses with a bold speech.'

'I wish you had. I spent a miserable day fretting and regretting stuff.'

'There wasn't really any way out of that. I wanted everyone here at breakfast tomorrow to surprise you,' he confided. 'I'm trying—not very well—to say I'm sorry for all the misunderstandings. I've never stopped loving you either. You took my sex drive with you when you married Luke.'

'I beg your pardon?' she whispered as he removed her necklace for her and she took off her earrings.

He unzipped her dress. 'I haven't been with anyone but you since I met you. Maybe that's why I was such a pushover in Italy,' he murmured with some defensiveness.

Scarlett whirled round, her eyes wide. 'Honestly...'

'I got burned with you and then I discovered that

I've outgrown casual affairs. I needed more and nobody came along who fitted the bill until you walked back into my life.'

'You *lured* me back into your life with that party invitation and I felt guilty about the twins and decided it was time to come clean—'

'And instead, we got down and dirty and it was amazing,' Aristide teased with a wicked grin as she tossed her dress on the bed and kicked off her heels before speeding into the dressing room to retrieve the dress she had worn on the beach almost three years earlier. 'I can't wait that long,' Aristide confided, removing the dress from her hold and drawing her close. 'I want to make love to you over and over again tonight.'

'Ambitious.' Scarlett ran her hands up over his muscular torso below his jacket and he tipped it off.

'Always. Also very turned on,' he confided in a roughened undertone. 'I love you, Scarlett. I love you so much that I will never give you up.'

'I love you too and you're not getting away either,' she whispered as he eased her down on the bed and then he was kissing her and talking died a natural death.

While he kissed her she was thinking about how he had attempted to recapture their original happiness by bringing her back to the island. Even before he'd fully accepted that he still loved her, he had attempted to restore what they had once had. And now that love, fully acknowledged between them for the very first time, was flaring up like a wildfire, sealing them together with fresh confidence and happiness.

Much later they escaped down to the beach, giving Marthe and her daughters the time and freedom to prepare the rooms for the family members due to arrive the next morning. After snacking on a late supper, they skinny-dipped in the shallows and then, damp and laughing, they ran up the steps and returned to their room, having decided that comfort and luxury were even better than reliving a memory to the authentic last note.

'I'd love another baby…some time,' he admitted as Scarlett blinked in surprise at that frank admission.

'Maybe next year,' she suggested, gazing down into emerald-green eyes that reflected all the love and appreciation she could ever hope to receive.

'You're amazing,' he told her appreciatively.

EPILOGUE

THREE YEARS LATER, Scarlett smoothed her dress down over her barely perceptible bump. She was five months into her second pregnancy and had stayed wonderfully small this time around because, mercifully, she was having a single baby. Rome and Alice were getting a little brother they planned to call Luca after Aristide's grandfather.

It was their third wedding anniversary and they were staging a fancy dinner to celebrate in London ahead of a trip to Dominica, where they would relax and enjoy being a couple, although she had already warned Aristide that he could forget the hiking trips.

Aristide was very excited about the baby, had accompanied her to every medical appointment and diligently provided his support in every way possible. He was a terrific father, which she hugely appreciated when his own father had set him such a poor example of fatherhood.

Riccardo Angelico had gradually become a regular part of their lives. He got on very well with Edith and Tom and, since his divorce, he and Aristide had had the freedom to get to know each other properly. Aristide had had to be honest about what he and his late twin had endured at Elisabetta's hands and Riccardo's unvarnished shock and dismay had done much to give father and son a better understanding of each other.

Elisabetta had given Aristide and Scarlett a very wide berth, refusing their invitation to attend their Italian church blessing. Scarlett had insisted on sending that invite but had not been too disappointed when Aristide's mother had turned them down. They had had a wonderful day and a party without her. Scarlett had been less certain of the right response when Elisabetta fell ill shortly after her husband divorced her.

The stress of the divorce, which she had contested at every opportunity, had left her with health problems and when she suffered a heart attack, it had been Scarlett who persuaded Aristide to visit her, even though he had been convinced that it was a false alarm, designed to bring him to heel. Unfortunately, heart surgery had not saved Elisabetta because she had passed away a few weeks afterwards from an unexpected complication.

Aristide had thanked Scarlett for persuading him to go to the hospital and make his peace with his mother. He had done it in his brother's name, moving on from the past and overcoming his own reluctance to go anywhere near the older woman. She had left her entire fortune and her jewellery to Aristide, which had been a surprise when Aristide had expected to be fully disinherited by her.

Rome and Alice were now sturdy four-year-olds, who talked a mile a minute and attended nursery school. Alice had stayed tiny while Rome grew and grew like Jack's beanstalk. He was crazy about football but Alice, who was a true tomboy, was even better at the game.

Scarlett no longer worked. During her pregnancy she had resigned, too tired to cope at school and have sufficient energy for her own children and Aristide.

Aristide walked through their bedroom door and said, 'I thought you were wearing a short dress tonight—'

'Not since my ankles swelled, so I put on a long one to hide them.'

Frowning, Aristide wrapped both arms round her and hugged her. 'You're gorgeous whatever you wear. But perhaps you should be taking it easier—'

'It's just the hot weather,' she argued.

'It'll be hotter on Dominica,' he reminded her.

Scarlett ran appreciative hands up under his jacket over his muscular chest. 'Yes, I'm looking forward to the skinny dipping already—'

'Not when you're pregnant.' Aristide shaped her protruding midriff. 'The bump is for my eyes only.'

'So, this is what you do. You get me pregnant and then start restricting my activities—'

'Not *all* of them,' Aristide asserted with a wicked

grin and a smoulderingly sexy appraisal that made heat curl in her pelvis. 'I'll skinny-dip…you get to watch—'

'Promises…promises,' she teased, gazing up at him with warm, adoring eyes, revelling in the way he hugged her with such ease, for the children had taught him the value of affection.

'I love you so much, *cara*.' Aristide extracted a long, lingering kiss that curled her toes and then raised his head again. 'Edith and Tom have arrived and they've taken the kids out to the garden.'

'Is this opportunity knocking?' she whispered.

'Afraid not…we've got to be horribly grown up and join them for drinks out there before dinner…but later, I will make you a very happy woman.'

'I'm already a very happy woman.'

'There's always room for more happiness. You taught me that.'

Scarlett smiled and clasped both his hands in hers. 'I love you, Mr Angelico.'

'Not half as much as I love you,' he told her with satisfaction.

* * * * *